"What buy you spying?"

"Incredible!" she breathed. "You're absolutely incredible! To think I felt a responsibility to warn you of spying within your own company!"

"I'm sure it was a big decision, making up your mind to come see me after you couldn't get enough out of your own employer." Holt moved a little closer, and on general principles Adena refused to take another step backward. "And if two thousand isn't enough, you're welcome to try bargaining for a bit more. I'll expect a little more in the way of usefulness out of you, naturally, if I do shell out a higher sum." The smoky eyes darkened as he raked her taut features. "But something tells me I might get my money's worth...."

Too late, Adena realized his intention. She put out her hands to ward him off, but it was useless. Strong fingers closed around her slender shoulders, and she was pulled effortlessly into his arms.

"No, damn it!" she snarled.

But her protest was cut off abruptly as Holt's warm, questing mouth came down on hers.

STEPHANIE JAMES

is a pseudonym for bestselling, award-winning author **Jayne Ann Krentz**. Under various pseudonyms—including Jayne Castle and Amanda Quick—Ms. Krentz has over 22 million copies of her books in print. Her fans admire her versatility as she switches between historical, contemporary and futuristic romances. She attributes a "lifelong addiction to romantic daydreaming" as the chief influence on her writing. With her husband, Frank, she currently resides in the Pacific Northwest.

Jayne Ann Krentz
WRITING AS

Stephanie James

PRICE OF SURRENDER

Silhouette Books

Published by Silhouette Books
America's Publisher of Contemporary Romance

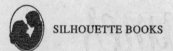

SILHOUETTE BOOKS

ISBN 0-373-80671-X

PRICE OF SURRENDER

Copyright © 1983 by Jayne Ann Krentz

Available Titles From
STEPHANIE JAMES

A PASSIONATE BUSINESS
DANGEROUS MAGIC
CORPORATE AFFAIR
STORMY CHALLENGE
VELVET TOUCH
LOVER IN PURSUIT
RENAISSANCE MAN
RECKLESS PASSION
PRICE OF SURRENDER
AFFAIR OF HONOR
GAMEMASTER
RAVEN'S PREY
SERPENT IN PARADISE
BATTLE PRIZE
BODY GUARD
GAMBLER'S WOMAN

And coming soon...

TO TAME THE HUNTER
THE SILVER SNARE
FABULOUS BEAST
NIGHT OF THE MAGICIAN
NIGHTWALKER
THE DEVIL TO PAY
WIZARD
GOLDEN GODDESS
CAUTIOUS LOVER
GREEN FIRE
SECOND WIFE
THE CHALLONER BRIDE

With love to my mother, Alberta,
who taught me about things like goals and being
willing to work for them. Hi, Mom! It's me!

One

Adena West stood pensively at the curving window of the dimly lit study and gazed out across San Francisco Bay. In the distance the San Francisco skyline sparkled like an exotic necklace in the night. The fog had not yet rolled in to shroud the lively city.

From her vantage point in the elegantly modern hillside home she could look down on the charming village of Sausalito. Located at the northern end of the Golden Gate Bridge, the whole town reminded Adena of an expensive, exotic Riviera resort with its sprawling homes clinging to the hills and its chic shops and restaurants clustered along the shore.

She loved it, as did almost everyone else who

visited Sausalito. Of course, she thought with a smile, she loved San Francisco, too, and she wouldn't be unhappy to drive back home across the bridge tonight as soon as her business was completed.

In fact, the business ahead of her was sufficiently unpleasant as to make her almost oblivious to the picturesque scene visible from the study window. She just wanted to get it over with and return home, where she could begin thinking about the changes this day had made in her life. The interview with Holt Sinclair was the last item on the day's unfortunate agenda. Once it was over, she could start looking ahead. Bleak as the future appeared at the moment, it would have to be faced sooner or later.

Adena was so wrapped up in her thoughts that she didn't hear the study door open behind her. It was the light suddenly flooding the room that brought her around with a quick grace.

"Miss West?" The man who had just entered and switched on the light stood studying her for a moment. "I'm Holt Sinclair. I understand you wanted to see me."

Adena nodded once, crisply, summing up the man in front of her with unexpected awareness. She had never met Holt Sinclair, but somehow he didn't fit the image she'd conceived.

For one thing, she realized abstractedly, he was

younger than she'd expected. Probably around thirty-seven or thirty-eight. His dark hair was brushed carelessly back from his broad forehead in a thick wave that was just beginning to show a sprinkling of silver.

From across the room his curiously smoky gray eyes met hers in a cool, speculative glance that told Adena she was being analyzed quite thoroughly. There was a hardness, a lean, unsparing toughness about the man which made her uneasy and set her nerves on edge.

No, that was just her imagination, Adena told herself firmly. Her nerves had been on edge all day. It hadn't taken this man's presence to create the uneasiness in her. Nevertheless, her wary response to Holt Sinclair seemed to heighten her senses in a way which couldn't be readily explained.

For the first time, Adena wondered if her mission tonight had been entirely unnecessary, after all. She had come to give this man a warning and she was beginning to doubt whether Holt Sinclair would need it.

There was a hard-edged, experienced cut to his aggressively carved features. His strong, straight nose and forceful jawline were grimly complemented by brackets of experience around his rather sensitive-looking mouth and the small lines at the corners of his gray eyes. Not a handsome face but one that carried the uncompromising stamp of masculinity in a way which struck the senses.

He was wearing a button-down plaid flannel shirt and khaki slacks that emphasized the width of his smoothly muscled shoulders and the tight leanness of his flat stomach and strong thighs.

Adena drew in her breath, vaguely appalled at the impact he'd made on her. She was here on business, she reminded herself deliberately. She would never see this man again after tonight.

"I'm Adena West," she began in her slightly throaty voice, a voice made even more husky tonight by the strain of the day just past.

"So my housekeeper said. Won't you have a seat?" Holt Sinclair moved across the room in a long, gliding stride, indicating the modern, round black chair on his left. He took the black leather seat behind the red enameled desk and waited with cool politeness.

Adena tried to ignore the continued speculation in his smoky gray eyes. She knew what he saw as she sank into her chair. It was the image reflected back at her from the ornately framed mirror behind his desk.

That image was of a woman who had recently turned twenty-eight. A woman with hair a rich umber shade which she wore parted simply in the middle. The dark blond hair curved heavily just below her chin, framing turquoise eyes and a face which would be labeled interesting before it was ever called beautiful.

The firm line of her nose and delicately forceful chin were softened by a full mouth and slightly slanting turquoise eyes, but the combination could not be termed traditionally lovely. The strength of character underneath could not be hidden, and the intelligence in the blue-green eyes held an attraction all its own. But both qualities were reserved for the more discerning eye. To those who failed to see it, the overall effect Adena West presented to the world was one of pleasant attractiveness.

It was an attractiveness which she augmented with a sense of style. Tonight the short, fitted, cognac suede jacket worn over a teal blue skirt proclaimed subtle, casual elegance. The teal and cinnamon-checked blouse framed the line of her throat with a short, stand-up collar. A burnished copper belt added a rakish sophistication which Adena wore well. The entire outfit clung gently to her slender figure, which had about it a certain betraying softness at the hips and breasts.

"I'm sorry to bother you at home like this," she plunged in determinedly, "but your secretary said it would be impossible to see you today at the office."

"And your business couldn't wait?" One sable brow lifted quizzically.

"I'm afraid not. Mr. Sinclair, I work..." Adena hesitated and then decided not to go into such details as the fact that she had just quit her job. "I work for Carrigan Labs."

"Ah! My competitors," he drawled with a smile that did nothing to lighten the smoky quality of his eyes. "Don't tell me Brad Carrigan has gotten desperate enough to try a little primitive bribery?"

Adena's eyes narrowed as she studied the cool mockery on his hard face. Perhaps she'd been wrong in thinking she had a duty to warn Holt Sinclair. Perhaps he deserved to be left to his fate!

"Mr. Sinclair," she told him in a soft tone which would have alerted anyone who knew her well. "I have had a very difficult day, to put it mildly. I am not in the mood for your chauvinistic jokes."

"Which means you're not the bribe? Pity. Something tells me you would have enlivened my average business day considerably." He got to his feet and moved to the polished black teak bar in the corner of the room. "Since you seem intent on discussing less interesting matters, we might as well do so in a civilized fashion."

Adena waited impatiently as Holt poured two small brandies and handed her one. She accepted it, knowing it would only delay matters further if she refused, but as soon as he'd placed it in her hand she set it down on the red enamel desk and forgot about it.

"It's really very good brandy," Holt coaxed dryly.

"I'm sure it is, but I'm not here to socialize. If you don't mind, Mr. Sinclair..."

"Call me Holt." He swirled the brandy once in the glass and sipped contemplatively.

"Thank you," she replied automatically, thinking it didn't matter very much what she called him. She would never be seeing him again. "Now, if you don't mind, I would like to get this over and done with. I have been working as an accountant for Carrigan Labs for about a year and..."

"Does Carrigan know you're here?" Holt interrupted amicably.

"No."

"I had about decided as much," he sighed. "Go on."

Adena frowned, not understanding but sensing things would get even more complicated if she asked him what he meant. "As I was saying, I've been working as an accountant with the firm for almost a year. Recently I began noticing some rather strange expenditures which didn't quite fit the normal pattern...."

His mouth twisted in a wryly amused smile.

"There's nothing like an accountant on the lookout for unexplained expenditures."

Adena shut her eyes briefly in exasperation. When she opened them again, it was to find Holt Sinclair watching her in a speculative fashion that totally belied his flippancy. In that instant she realized that regardless of what he said, she had his full attention.

"I'll be as brief as I can about this, Mr. Sinclair."

"Holt."

"As far as I was able to determine, the unusual expenditures were kickback payments being made to a high-ranking member of your own firm!"

If she had expected to astound and shock him, she was in for a surprise. Holt merely took another lingering sip of the brandy and waited for her to go on.

"I...I didn't have genuine proof, you understand," she continued a little uncertainly, not understanding his apparent lack of interest. "It would take a full-scale audit to turn that up, but I had enough to...to confront my boss."

"You went to Brad Carrigan with your little discovery?"

"No, my immediate manager is his son Jeff," Adena told him distantly, remembering the ensuing scene which had concluded not only with the loss of her job but of a personal relationship she had begun to think might lead to something important.

She didn't honestly know whether the unhappiness she felt was due to her discovery of Jeff Carrigan's low standard of business and personal integrity or her own failure to see that aspect of him earlier in their relationship.

"And what was Jeff Carrigan's reaction?" With the softness of the question, Adena suddenly became aware of how Holt's dark, drawling voice ruffled her nerve endings. For some reason it brought images of the depths of the sea into her mind. Dark, deep and potentially dangerous.

'He…he confirmed…Mr. Sinclair, I don't want to go into details about that end of things. Suffice it to say that there is every reason to believe Carrigan Labs has been paying off one of your SinTech employees to the tune of several thousand dollars. As far as I can tell, it is an employee connected with your thin film coating materials division. I think that person is selling your industrial secrets to Carrigan Labs."

Adena finished in a little rush, glad to have the worst over. Only a stern sense of duty had brought her here tonight, and now that it had been appeased, she wanted nothing more than to go home and recover from what undoubtedly would rank as one of the worst days of her life.

Holt was no longer watching her as intently. His gaze was focused on the contents of his glass as if he sought some information from the brandy. When he looked up at last, it was with a look that seemed to impale her like a butterfly on a pin.

"You said Brad Carrigan doesn't know you're here tonight. What about his son?"

"Jeff doesn't know I'm here, either," she murmured.

"I see." There was a short pause and then Holt asked smoothly, "I'd like to hear a little more about what the younger Carrigan said when you confronted him with the news."

"I'd rather not discuss it."

He nodded as if he fully understood. "But whatever was said between the two of you, the end result is that you came here tonight to offer me the same information."

Adena frowned, thinking that was a strange way to phrase it. "I'm telling you what I learned because I felt you had a right to know."

"Very commendable of you. Won't you at least try the brandy, Adena?"

She glanced at the still-full glass and with a small shrug beneath her suede jacket, she reached out to lift the glass off the red desk. Her terra-cotta colored nails contrasted with the brandy in the crystal. Dutifully she sipped, her eyes meeting Holt's enigmatic ones over the rim.

He lifted one dark brow as a silent comment on

the tiny sips she had taken. "I can understand why an accountant, of all people, would wish to keep a clear head when dealing with high finance. But you really don't have to worry, Adena. I'm a fair man."

"I'm sure you are," she said resolutely. "Now, if you'll excuse me, I'll be on my way. I'm sorry I can't give you the name of the person in your organization who is selling your secrets, but perhaps you'll be able to plug the leak now that you know it's there."

She got gracefully to her feet, reaching for the small, copper-trimmed leather purse beside her. At long last she was free to go home and unwind after the traumatic day. She really shouldn't have had even that one sip of brandy on an empty stomach, she mused.

"You don't have to worry about supplying all the details, Adena," Holt murmured, rising behind the desk politely. "I already have the name of the man selling SinTech's secrets."

"What!" She whirled to face him, shocked.

He nodded with a curious smile. "But I don't want you to think I'm not properly appreciative of the information you brought me. Please sit down and finish your drink."

She stared at him, thoroughly shaken. When she thought of all she had been through today and then to have him quietly say he knew everything...

It was, she decided, sinking back into the black chair and reaching determinedly for the brandy, a fitting end to an incredibly bad day! Without a word, she took another, much healthier sip of brandy, holding her breath as it burned its way down to her stomach.

Holt eyed her reproachfully as she set the crystal glass down with great care. "I wanted you to enjoy it, of course, but I didn't mean you had to guzzle it."

Adena caught her breath as the brandy finally hit bottom. She shot her host a cold, disgusted glance. "You knew? All along?"

"He's one of my engineers at the thin materials research and development lab," Holt told her simply. "He's been selling information to Carrigan Labs for three months. My congratulations on having picked up on it so quickly." He lifted his brandy glass in salute. "You must be quite good at your job."

"When did you...? How did you find out?" she whispered.

"I discovered it shortly after he began," he explained, lifting one broad shoulder in easy dismissal. "I decided to let it continue until I had the proof I needed to fire the man. In the meantime, I've made sure that he's no longer involved with critical research projects."

Adena focused on the brandy remaining in her glass. Only a perverted sense of humor could find anything amusing about this whole mess, she decided grimly. But there was a certain wry irony in it, she told herself as she took another sip and thought about the day's disasters.

"Well," she announced with a self-mocking little smile, "it would appear I've wasted my time coming here tonight. I'm sorry I disturbed your evening, Mr. Sinclair. I won't keep you any longer."

"Please don't get the idea I'm ungrateful, Adena," he countered softly. His smoky gray eyes gave her a very level glance. "I intend to show my appreciation for your efforts tonight."

She blinked, not understanding but sensing trouble. "There's nothing to thank me for. I did what I felt I had to do and now I'd like to go home." She wished the brandy fumes weren't swirling in her head. She really should have eaten something earlier...

"Have you had dinner?" Holt asked perceptively as her terra-cotta nails tightened on the arm of her chair.

She shook her head. "There wasn't time. I wanted to come here first and get the whole thing over with as quickly as possible."

"I can understand that. Your first venture into this sort of thing?"

She eyed him morosely, deciding it was the brandy which was making his conversation become less and less intelligible. "I suppose you could say that," she finally agreed carefully.

He nodded. "I understand. I expect it's always difficult the first time. And I didn't make things easier for you by spoiling your little surprise, did I? But I insist you stay and have a bite to eat with me. My housekeeper will have left by now, but she always prepares enough for two before she leaves for the evening. Won't you join me? To be honest, I think you should at least give the brandy time to wear off before you drive home."

He was already on his feet, coming around from behind the red desk in a lithe, purposeful stride that seemed to catch her up and sweep her along. Before she quite realized what was happening, Adena found herself being escorted out of the red-black-and-beige study down a hall to a large, modern kitchen.

On the way she had a brief glimpse of a spacious living room which seemed to continue the color scheme she'd encountered in the study. A golden beige carpet served as backdrop for the rich impact of black and red furniture and accessories. The floor-to-ceiling windows took full advantage of the Bay view.

In the kitchen the red predominated on counter surfaces and appliances, but the effect was lightened by the use of white tile on the floor and sparing touches of black. A small circular table and its two small chairs, in fact, were about the only evidence of the darker shade.

"Mr. Sinclair," Adena began in an effort to retrieve some control over the situation, "this is very kind of you, but I don't..."

"Nonsense, I'm never kind. And the name is Holt, remember?"

She watched a little helplessly as he released her and strode over to the built-in oven. "What have we here?" He sniffed as he opened the door and smiled in satisfaction. "A quiche. Which means, if I'm not mistaken, a salad somewhere. Annie always serves a salad with her spinach quiche." He walked over to the refrigerator and opened it expectantly. "Just as I thought," he declared, removing a bowl of mixed greens. "Would you mind getting down the plates? They're in that cupboard over there."

Feeling as if she were being adroitly maneuvered, but unable to figure out a logical reason to halt the manipulation, Adena obediently set the black table by the bay window. A little food probably wasn't a bad idea, she told herself determinedly as Holt brought the meal across the room and waved her into a chair.

"We'll eat first and then finish our business," he

said negligently, handing Adena a knife with which to slice the quiche while he tossed the salad.

"There doesn't seem to be a great deal more to discuss," she managed to point out as she took a bite of the spinach quiche. Whoever Annie was, she was a good cook. Adena appreciated good cooking.

"Of course there is. You mustn't be so self-deprecating or you won't make a success of this sort of thing." Holt smiled a little coolly as he picked up his fork.

"I don't quite understand, Holt. What exactly are you trying to say?"

"Never mind. We'll talk after dinner. Now have some of Annie's salad and tell me something about yourself."

That surprised her. "What do you want to know?"

"I'm making casual conversation, can't you tell? How about telling me where you live? What you do when you're not busy accounting, what sort of films you like. The usual introductory sort of thing."

"I can't imagine why you're interested," she murmured dryly. The food was certainly hitting the spot.

"I told you, I'm being polite."

"Okay, I live in San Francisco, I like good food and I rarely go to films. I prefer to read in the evenings. Is that enough or would you like to know my astrological sign and who I voted for in the last election?''

''A bit sharp-tongued, too, I see.''

Adena drew a long breath, seeking patience again. ''I'm sorry. I'm on edge today.''

''And I've told you I understand. Stop worrying. It's all going to work out, you know. You have nothing to worry about,'' he soothed mildly.

Nothing to worry about! What a laugh! Adena smiled a bit grimly. ''If you say so.''

''I'm saying so. Do you want leftover chocolate mousse for dessert or lemon curd tart?''

''Annie seems to take good care of you.''

''She should. I pay her enough to take excellent care of my home,'' he drawled.

''You get what you pay for, I suppose,'' Adena retorted, trying for the same light dryness in her voice. Holt Sinclair was beginning to sound like a rather cynical man. But perhaps that was to be expected from someone so successful.

''I've always believed that,'' he said with quiet emphasis. ''And I'm fortunate enough to be in a position to pay for just about everything I need or want.''

Adena raised one umber brow as she forked up the last of her salad. ''Congratulations,'' she muttered.

"Thank you. Now did you want the lemon tart or the leftover mousse?"

"I think I'll have the tart."

He nodded. "You're beginning to look a little better already."

"I didn't know I was looking that wretched to begin with!" she snapped, annoyed.

He laughed, a deep rich sound that somehow struck her as almost sensuous. "Not wretched, just a bit frayed around the edges." He got to his feet to clear the table and she automatically rose to help him.

"As I said, it's been a hard day."

"Yes. But it's over, so you can relax. Come on, we'll eat these in the living room." Without waiting for her approval, Holt picked up two small lemon tarts and started out the kitchen door.

Once again Adena couldn't think of anything else to do but follow along. This was getting ridiculous! She was beginning to feel like a small, faithful dog. Which reminded her. She hoped her neighbor had remembered to take Max out this evening.

"What are you smiling at?" he inquired interestedly, setting the tarts down on a glass-topped coffee table in front of a curving, black couch.

"I was thinking I'm starting to feel like my schnauzer, Max, must when he follows me around in hopes of getting fed."

Holt chuckled as she sat down beside him, ignoring the careful distance she put between them. "I suppose dogs have their price, too, same as everyone and everything else. With them it's food."

"I'm getting the impression you have a well-developed capitalist view of life!" The tart was delicious, the *pâté brisée* crust light and flaky.

"And I have the distinct impression our views of life aren't so very different," he murmured softly.

Adena paused thoughtfully after taking a mouthful of tart, swallowed, and then asked very cautiously, "Exactly what is that supposed to mean?"

"Only that your visit tonight won't be wasted."

A horrible suspicion began to form in her mind. Deliberately she cut another piece of tart with her fork. "Not wasted? When you already knew about the information I had to bring you?"

Holt set his plate down on the glass table and lounged back into the cushions, eyeing her appraisingly. Adena sat tensely on the edge of the couch, waiting.

"I wouldn't want you to think me ungrateful, Adena," he said gently.

"I see," she whispered remotely. "And just how grateful did you intend to be?"

Thoroughly disgusted with herself for having ever felt obliged to warn Holt Sinclair about the leak in his company, Adena silently wondered how she could have been such a fool. The man certainly hadn't needed her help! Furthermore, even if he had been unaware of the payoffs, it struck her rather forcibly that she needn't have felt any sense of responsibility toward him. Holt Sinclair, she decided a bit late, could take care of himself!

"I expect I'll prove grateful to the tune of about two thousand," he said matter-of-factly, watching her through slightly narrowed eyes.

"Two thousand!" She stared at him, appalled.

"Well, you have to remember you were bringing me old news, Adena," he drawled.

"Two thousand dollars? You'd pay me that for what I told you tonight?"

"Look, I don't know what you've been led to believe, but the new business you're entering tonight isn't exactly going to provide you with windfall profits. At least, not in the beginning and not with old information. And a bit of advice on the negotiating, while I'm at it. It's best not to give away your product until you've made the deal."

Adena leaped to her feet, her shocked face infused with a high flush of anger. "I don't believe this!"

"What's the matter? Did Carrigan offer you more than that to keep silent? If he did, tell me. I'm willing to up the ante in order to keep the lines of communication open. Who knows? In the future you might come up with something even more worthwhile.''

Adena backed away automatically as Holt came up off the couch in an easy, coordinated movement. She couldn't take her eyes off him. It was like being fascinated with a cobra, she decided fleetingly.

''Just how high,'' she managed tightly, ''are you willing to go?''

''That depends,'' he murmured thoughtfully, taking a step forward. ''What would it take to buy your loyalty?''

''Incredible!'' she breathed. ''You're absolutely incredible! To think I felt a responsibility to *warn* you! When I think of what I've been through today...!''

''I'm sure it was a big decision, making up your mind to come to me after you couldn't get enough out of Carrigan.'' Holt moved a little closer but Adena refused to take another step backward. ''And if two thousand isn't enough, you're welcome to try bargaining for a bit more. I'll expect a little more in the way of usefulness out of you, naturally, if I do shell out a much higher sum.'' His smoky eyes darkened as he raked her taut features. ''But something tells me I might get my money's worth...''

Too late, Adena realized his intention. She threw up her hands to ward him off, but it was useless Strong fingers closed around the cognac suede covering her slender shoulders and she was pulled effortlessly into his arms.

"No, damn it!" she hissed.

But her protest was cut off abruptly as Holt's warm, questing mouth came down on hers.

Two

Instinctively Adena stood absolutely rigid as Holt explored her mouth. She sensed almost immediately that there was no overwhelming danger of further assault from him. It was as if he only wanted a sampling of whatever lay beneath the surface. It was, she decided, thoroughly annoying to be tasted as if one were a piece of fruit being tested for ripeness!

His strong, capable hands moved slightly on her shoulders in a subtle, kneading action as he deepened the exploration of her mouth. Adena felt the coaxing persuasive movement of his lips as he molded hers in a dampening, deliberately sensuous contact.

"Relax, honey," he commanded enticingly without lifting his mouth from hers, "we'll work something out. I'm not an unreasonable man…"

"I agree," she got out between gritted teeth. "I was the unreasonable one to think I had an obligation to bring my information to you!"

"Why are you so upset? I'm willing to pay…"

"Two thousand dollars?" she grated furiously.

'Not enough? Under the circumstances, I thought that was rather generous!"

"You're impossible. Will you kindly let me go? We have nothing more to discuss."

"I think we do. I'm willing to bet you have a lot more to offer than just some old information. There's something about you which intrigues me, Adena West, and I'm willing to pay for what amuses me."

Her turquoise eyes burned with fires of resentment as they met the smoky-gray ones examining her. There was no point trying to argue or reason with the man. He was just like Jeff—no, he was worse than Jeff because he didn't even bother with the pretense of polite maneuvering. Holt Sinclair simply assumed he could buy whatever he wanted or needed.

Holt's mouth curved subtly upward as he absorbed the anger in her and one hand left her shoulder. With deliberate sensuality he traced the outline of her mouth with his forefinger, pausing to probe gently at the corner until he had forced apart her lips.

Adena tried to wrench herself free as the erotic caress continued, this time along the sensitive inside of her lower lip.

"Let me go, damn it!"

He ignored the demand, bending his head to touch her now more vulnerable mouth with his tongue. Adena's hands splayed across his chest, her nails sinking into the fabric of his shirt as she pushed futilely against him.

But there was no stopping the intimate search he had begun.

"Let me inside, honey," he growled softly, tugging her closer. "Part your lips for me, Adena. I want a taste of what I'm getting."

"You're getting nothing from me, you bastard! I won't..."

Before she could finish the scathing sentence, he was inside, using the opportunity to slide his tongue aggressively between her teeth and into the dark warmth of her mouth. The kiss abruptly became more than a sampling, exploring caress. Much more.

Adena felt her breath catch in her throat as the impact of the suddenly marauding, dominating caress swept over her in a wave. It shook her in a manner she wouldn't have believed possible, making her unexpectedly weak.

Helplessly she used the fingers with which she had been trying to push him away to steady herself instead. She knew he must be aware of the effect he was having on her faltering defenses. He was too good a businessman not to know, she decided wrathfully.

Telling herself that her only rational response was to let him play out his scene of masculine dominance until she had a chance to get free, Adena tried to stand passively beneath the ocean breaker which was foaming over her and tossing her about as if she were so much flotsam on the tide.

Predictably enough, perhaps, as soon as he sensed her unwillingness to engage in outright battle, Holt's tactics changed. He didn't relinquish the hard-won territory of her mouth but there was a subtle shift in his pattern of exploration. His tongue probed more gently, urging hers to respond, and his lips slid moistly over hers in a persuasive manner.

Adena stiffened when his hand moved to encircle the nape of her neck and hold her in place for the remainder of the kiss. But she didn't try to fight him; she merely waited.

At long last he lifted his head with obvious reluctance but with equally obvious satisfaction. His gray eyes gleamed down at her softened mouth and resentful gaze.

"Something tells me you and I are going to work very well together," he murmured deeply, his hand still toying absently with her hair.

Adena refused to be goaded into saying anything. She stood mutely, waiting for an opportunity to escape.

"Don't look so sulky, sweetheart," he went on in amusement. "I'll make it all worth your while."

"Are you quite finished?" Adena finally said in an amazingly calm voice. "May I leave now?"

He smiled with teasing mockery. "Are you sure you want to run off so soon?"

"Quite sure!"

"But we have so much to talk about," he growled with suppressed laughter. His gray eyes were warmer now than they had been when she'd first met him in the study, Adena thought vaguely. There was a heat in his gaze which could only be attributed to the incipient flames of passion.

For the first time, she experienced a twinge of genuine fear. It was definitely time to get out of Holt Sinclair's reach.

"Perhaps," she whispered very daringly, knowing she needed a small diversion, "if you were to write out that check for two thousand…?"

"Of course." He nodded at once. She felt the

satisfaction in him and could have struck him. "I can understand how you would feel more comfortable knowing I'm a man of my word."

Adena was appalled at the cynicism which sharpened his gray eyes as he turned away and strode toward the study. My God, she thought wonderingly. He really did think he could buy anything! It was a little staggering. She shook her head in an unconscious gesture of incomprehension and picked up her purse.

Well, she had learned her lesson. Tough, hardbitten men like Holt Sinclair didn't need people like her feeling any sense of responsibility toward them. They could take care of themselves! She watched him disappear down the hall to the study and then turned unhesitatingly toward the front door.

Once safely outside, Adena didn't waste a second. She was into her bright yellow Audi and on her way down the winding hills toward the Golden Gate Bridge in record time. One could only give thanks that such disastrous days were usually infrequent occurrences in the course of a lifetime!

It wasn't until she turned the key in the lock of her flat and heard Max's cheerful bark of welcome that Adena finally began to relax. As she opened the door, her handsome, standard-size schnauzer came forward with as much eagerness as his innate dignity would allow him to demonstrate.

"Oh, Max, you don't know how good it is to come home to a civilized, polite, and thoroughly admirable male such as yourself," Adena told him with a chuckle, leaning down to scratch behind his pointed gray ears.

Max lifted his mustachioed face for the caress, clearly happy to have her safely home.

"Just wait," she vowed, "until I've told you all about my day!"

With a sigh of relief, Adena crossed the small, plant-filled foyer and entered the living room of the flat. A rich persimmon carpet swept from one end to the bay windows which looked out onto the street. It served as a luscious backdrop for the predominately white and green color scheme.

Adena flung herself down on the white sofa, kicked off her shoes, and leaned back with a small groan. It was over. A great deal was over.

"I hope you don't mind eating an inferior grade of dog food for a while, Max." She thought about her finances in the light of her unemployed state. There should be enough in her savings to see her through a couple of months of job-hunting without forcing Max to eat that horrible dry dog food he detested. If worse came to worse, she could start liquidating her small stock account.

But, she told herself with forced cheer, it shouldn't be too long before she got another position. She was a well-trained and fairly experienced accountant. Surely she wouldn't find herself pounding the streets for long?

Adena glanced over at her copy of the *Wall Street Journal* and thought about checking the employment ads. No, tomorrow would be soon enough to start. Tonight she needed some sleep.

"You'll be happy to know, Max, that you won't be seeing much of Jeff Carrigan anymore," she remarked in a tired voice. When Max pricked up his ears and pushed his nose into her lap, she smiled wryly. "I know you didn't like him very much. Today I became somewhat disenchanted with him myself!"

How badly was she going to miss Jeff Carrigan? It hadn't been a heartrending experience telling him not to bother calling her anymore. But it had been a depressing one. She had been attracted to his easy charm and their mutual interest in the field of accounting. He had been a handsome, polished escort whom she had begun to hope might have a place in her future. With her career well-established, Adena had told herself, the time had come to think about the future.

She closed her eyes briefly against the memory of Jeff's reaction to her discovery of the payoffs. He had smiled at her with a slightly cynical, wholly attractive smile, his tawny brown eyes faintly derisive, as he calmly explained the corporate facts of life.

"It's a competitive world, sweetheart," he'd soothed with a blatant sense of masculine superiority. "Carrigan Labs has to use any edge it can get."

"But this is wrong, Jeff!" she'd protested, sounding remarkably naive, even to herself, yet not knowing what else to do except argue. "It's stealing!"

"It's business," he'd corrected calmly.

"Does...does your father know?"

"He and I, together with a couple of others, are about the only ones who do know. Congratulations, sweetheart, you've just joined a very select group," Jeff had joked. "Lucky for everyone concerned you're almost a part of the family, hmmm?"

She'd lost her temper shortly after that, arguing heatedly that she wouldn't be a part of the scheme. He'd sat behind his massive walnut desk and let her "get it out of her system," as he put it.

When she'd finished, he calmly told her to go back to her office and leave the harder side of business to him. She'd stared at him for a long moment, knowing he wasn't going to put a stop to the payoff scheme, and knowing he fully expected her to ignore the unusual expenditures in her books.

Very coolly and very deliberately Adena had lifted her chin and told him not to call her again. The memory of the surprise on his handsome features was the only satisfaction she'd taken from the scene. She'd gone back to her office, typed out her resignation with an outward calm which amazed her, and left.

She should have stopped right there, Adena decided with the wisdom of hindsight. Whatever had possessed her to think she had an obligation to warn Holt Sinclair? She should have guessed he didn't need her help! But that offer to pay for it anyway...!

"Men!" She smiled down at the schnauzer reassuringly. "I'm not including you in that general indictment, Max."

Restlessly Adena got to her feet. Everything would look better in the morning, she decided. First things first, she consoled herself wandering into the bedroom with its white carpet and persimmon-and-green bed. Right now she needed sleep.

The next morning she picked up several newspapers as she took Max out for his walk. By the time she returned to her apartment, Adena felt invigorated and ready for the start which had to be made. It was incredible, she thought as she carefully selected her morning tea, how one's whole life could change in the course of a day!

She deliberated briefly over her extensive collection of fine teas and finally chose the hearty English Breakfast blend. Poring over job ads was not a task to be tackled with the aid of a light and delicate tea.

It called for a mixture that would be assertive, to say the least!

She rinsed the lovely Chinese earthenware pot with hot water to preheat it, measured out a healthy amount of tea leaves, and poured in briskly boiling water. Tea was something Adena took very seriously.

She was in the process of breaking open a buttery croissant when the phone rang. Frowning, she reached across the small dining room table to answer it. The newspaper in her lap rustled.

As soon as she spoke a greeting, Adena wished she'd had the sense to take the phone off the hook. She should have guessed.

"Where the hell are you, Adena? It's nearly ten o'clock! I've been down to your office twice already this morning."

"Didn't you get my letter of resignation, Jeff?"

"Oh, that? I tore it up, naturally, as soon as it reached my desk. We both know you wrote it in the heat of anger. I must admit, I would never have expected such a temper in a mild-mannered little accountant!" Jeff Carrigan added with a flash of humor.

Adena was not amused. Yesterday had showed her a few things about herself besides the fact that she had a temper. She'd also apparently been blessed with a rather oversized dose of naiveté! But she was learning.

"I hate to break this to you, Jeff, but I meant every word of that resignation. I have no intention of working for a firm that expects me to ignore payoffs and kickbacks in my books."

Beside her chair Max lifted his head alertly as her voice tightened with tension. Good old Max. The one male Adena knew who would always be willing to leap to her defense!

"Adena, calm down. It's obvious you're still upset. Look, sweetheart, take a couple of days off. Hell, take a week off. You've got it coming, and I'll handle things in Personnel for you. As far as the records will show, you're on vacation. In a few days, when you've calmed down, you can come back to work and no one here will be the wiser."

"Good-bye, Jeff."

"And another thing, darling," he added just as if he hadn't heard her crisp farewell, "I seem to have come into possession of a pair of tickets for that new show that opened last week." His voice deepened with affectionate humor. "Any idea what I should do with them? A shame to waste…"

"Turn them into Lost and Found!"

Adena hung up the phone with a clatter and then immediately started dialing the number of the Carrigan Labs Personnel Department. So Jeff had torn up her resignation, had he?

Ten minutes later she had made her departure from the company very official. Her resignation would be explained as having been handed in for "personal reasons." Carol Walters, the assistant director of Personnel, didn't seem to think Adena was acting irrationally. She accepted the resignation and said she'd cut the paperwork immediately.

"We're all going to miss you, Adena," the older woman had remarked. "Keep in touch, won't you?"

Not if I can help it, Adena thought unhappily and hung up the phone. She turned back to the want ads with great resolution. After she'd marked a few of the more interesting openings she would have to get her résumé updated.

It was two days later that the new résumés went into the mail, however, and during that time Adena did some serious thinking about Jeff Carrigan's suggestion. Perhaps she should take some time off while she waited for responses to the résumés. When she returned, she could start following up with phone calls and personal visits. She had no intention of taking the remainder of his advice and returning to work at Carrigan Labs, of course, but the idea of a short vacation appealed to her.

She thought about it while preparing dinner,

which she carried out into the living room to eat in front of the evening news on the third night of her unemployment.

"What do you think, Max?" she inquired during a commercial. "We could go someplace restful and quaint. A friend of mine in the accounting department at work was telling me about this lovely old inn in one of the old gold rush towns up in the mother lode region. Would you like that?"

Max, basically a refined city dog at heart, considered her question carefully. He still hadn't given a clear answer when the doorbell chimed, saving him from having to do so.

With a sigh, Adena put down the needlework she had been doing half-heartedly while she ate and watched t.v. and rose to answer the door. She really wasn't in the mood for visitors, she decided irritably as she padded across the persimmon rug. The soft ballet-style slippers she was wearing made no sound as she crossed to the intercom box and depressed the talk button. The bateau neck of her slightly oversized emerald sweater slid off one shoulder in an alluring fashion of which she was unaware at the moment. She had put on the overscale sweater and the spare white pants strictly for her own comfort that evening.

"Yes?"

"Adena? It's Holt Sinclair."

Adena released the talk button as if it had become electrified. Holt Sinclair? What in the world was he doing on her doorstep? For some reason his deep voice came as more of a nerve-ruffling shock than it should have. Her reaction to it was far stronger than Adena wanted to admit.

"How unfortunate," she managed to reply.

"Your warmth of welcome is overwhelming. May I please come in?"

"Why?" she demanded.

"I want to talk to you."

"The feeling isn't particularly mutual. I don't think we have anything to discuss, Mr. Sinclair, and I'm occupied at the moment. So would you please go away?"

There was a short pause before the dark voice came back over the intercom. "You have someone with you?" The strangely neutral tone was curiously alarming.

"Yes, as a matter of fact, I do." Adena smiled grimly across the room at Max.

"Not Jeff Carrigan, I trust?" Holt murmured coolly.

Adena started, wondering why he should ask about Jeff. "No, his name is Max, since you're interested. Good night, Mr. Sinclair."

"Max? How interesting," he drawled. "You certainly don't waste any time, do you?"

Adena frowned ferociously at the intercom box. "I beg your pardon?"

"I mean that for a young woman who just broke off a serious relationship three days ago, you're certainly not letting any grass grow..."

"How do you know about that?" Adena demanded in an angry gasp.

"Let me in and I'll tell you. Actually, I know a great deal more about you than that. Don't worry, I'll be civilized toward Max. I've come to apologize, Adena," he added on a gentler, more persuasive note.

"That's not necessary..."

"Adena, please. I made a mistake. The least you can do is let me apologize properly. Besides, it's awfully cold out here in this fog," he added a little plaintively.

Adena knew she was weakening. Damn it, there was something about that voice...!

"All right," she surrendered ungraciously. "You can come in for a moment but I want your word you won't be difficult when I ask you to leave. Is that understood?"

"Yes, ma'am."

In spite of herself, Adena smiled at the humble response. If ever there was a man who had a hard time with humility, it was Holt Sinclair.

He came through her door a moment later, filling

it with a darkly masculine presence that contrasted in a vivid, totally virile manner with the light, luscious persimmon, white and green room. The fog had dampened his sable dark hair and seemed to have become part of the smoky eyes Adena remembered so well. He was wearing a coffee-brown suede jacket over a heathery sweater and brown slacks. At the sight of him, Adena questioned her decision to let him in.

Max came forward alertly—examining, analyzing, and assessing. He stood looking up at the stranger, and before Adena could make introductions, Holt reached down with a grin to stroke the dog's gray head.

"Hello, Max," Holt said cheerfully.

Adena raised her eyes heavenwood. So much for that small ploy.

"Let me take your jacket," she offered politely, watching as he shrugged out of it obediently. "Would you like some tea?"

"Sounds terrific." Holt handed her the jacket, his gray eyes sweeping the room with more than casual interest. "Something tells me your decorator wouldn't get along at all with the one who did my place. Did you choose Max because his gray fur looked good against that carpet?"

"No, I chose the carpet to go with his fur! For heaven's sake, Holt, what a thing to say. If Max could understand, he'd have every reason to be offended! Just because your designer was obviously a minimalist who liked dramatic effects…''

"He said it was a *masculine* effect." Holt grinned in humorous protest. "And on second thought, maybe your designer would get along with mine. If ever there was a more feminine room…I assume a woman did it?"

"Have a seat," she instructed briskly, striving instinctively to put an end to that subject. "I'll get another cup and saucer."

She watched him lower himself to the white couch where she had been sitting, reach over and turn off the television set as if he were right at home, and then turn his attention to her meal.

"Hungry?" she inquired forbiddingly.

"Starved," he admitted cheerfully. "But what kind of a meal is this?"

"I felt like having a West Country tea for dinner this evening. Any objections?" She dared him to complain.

He mused over the three-tiered silver stand with its delicate assortment of potted shrimp triangles, cucumber sandwiches cut in dainty rounds, and long, thin, anchovy toasts. To one side a tiny treacle tart sat in solitary splendor near the bone china teapot.

"None at all," he assured her, reaching for one

of the potted shrimp triangles. "Except that I could wolf all this down in about two minutes flat."

"You will be depriving me of my dinner if you do!"

"Is this all there is?"

"I wasn't expecting company!"

"I should have given you advance warning. You could have put together a few more cucumber sandwiches," he apologized around a mouthful of the shrimp triangle.

Making a commendable effort to hang on to her temper, Adena marched into the kitchen, collected another of the delicate, flower-trimmed tea cups and spread some more potted shrimp on a couple of man-sized pieces of bread. There was also, unfortunately, another treacle tart left in the refrigerator. She had made an extra one for her lunch the following day. Oh, well.

When she walked back into the living room a few minutes later it was to find Max lounging regally at Holt Sinclair's feet, graciously accepting a bite of crunchy anchovy toast.

"Trying to bribe my dog?" she murmured with unthinking flippancy.

"Since I didn't have much luck bribing his owner, I thought I'd give it a shot." At the sight of her suddenly taut expression, Holt groaned. "I'm sorry, Adena. Bad joke."

"But it wasn't a joke, was it?" she retorted crisply, setting down the large sandwich and the extra tart. "You meant every word of it that night." She poured the Formosa Oolong tea into his cup with casual grace and then pointedly took the green and persimmon print chair across from him. She had no intention of sharing the couch.

He slanted her a glance that held the same sort of speculation he'd viewed her with the night she'd gone to his home to warn him. But instead of commenting on the subject of bribery, he put out a large hand to finger the cascade of green material which Adena had left in a heap on the couch when she'd risen to answer the door.

"What is it?" he queried lightly, picking up the small portion of the material which had been stretched tightly over a round embroidery hoop. Stitches done in jewel-toned crewel yarn had begun to fill in the traced design of birds sitting on branches of a stylized tree.

"Eventually it's going to be a table cloth," Adena told him, sipping at her tea.

"Eventually?"

"I've been working on it for a year," she confessed dryly. "I'll probably still be working on it next year."

"Just as well," he chuckled. "It's a hobby that

goes very nicely with this room and with Max and with high tea."

"Holt..."

"I know. You want your apology," he sighed, picking up his teacup. "And I do apologize. But how was I to guess you weren't looking for a few bucks that night? I mean, it was the logical assumption to make, given the circumstances..."

"Was it?" she said skeptically.

"Adena, please," he soothed. "How was I to know you'd given up both a job and a boyfriend before coming to me that night?"

"Speaking of which," she bit out caustically, "how do you happen to know those facts now?"

"I called your office. There seemed to be a little confusion, but it finally became apparent you had resigned. There was no confusion at all about the relationship being over. I got the full story in juicy detail!"

"From whom?" Adena snapped, thoroughly annoyed.

"From the head of your old department, who had it directly from the lips of Jeff Carrigan's secretary," he told her triumphantly.

"With the flow of information back and forth between Carrigan Labs and SinTech, it's a wonder the two don't simply decide to merge!" Adena muttered bitterly.

He ignored that, his mouth firming. "Adena, I made a hell of a mistake that night. I handled things very badly. But I had no idea you'd gone out on a limb like that before coming to me with your information. I admire the fact that you didn't approach me until you'd severed your ties with Carrigan. And I freely admit it was an insult to offer you a couple of thousand dollars for the news you brought me. After all, you'd just abandoned your livelihood! Not to mention a man who could have taken care of you rather nicely…"

"Holt, this 'apology' is beginning to sound a bit strange," Adena warned dangerously.

"I'm sorry. I should make myself clear. Adena, I'm here to offer you the only thing that can adequately compensate you for what you abandoned when you left Carrigan Labs: a position with SinTech and a man who can take care of you. Me."

Three

For a long moment Adena simply stared at the man on her couch. His look of unconcerned assurance was absolutely fascinating. She watched as he finished a bite of sandwich and picked up his teacup. And then she shook her head in awed amazement.

"I do believe you really mean that," she finally said, setting her cup down with great care.

"I never say things I don't mean," he said easily, watching her face intently.

"I'll remember that." From somewhere deep inside an imp of mischief sprang awake. The man was too incredible to take seriously, she realized. "Your generosity is most flattering," she went on, her eyes lowered demurely to the contents of her teacup.

"I'm only sorry I wasn't sufficiently generous the other night. I would have been if you'd made your position clearer."

"My fault entirely," she agreed dryly. "As you noticed, I was a little new at the game."

There was a fractional beat in time during which she could sense Holt trying to decide whether or not she was being serious. She lifted her gaze to meet his smoky gray eyes and smiled brilliantly.

"Another cup of tea?"

"Thank you," he said automatically, a slight frown hardening the lines around his mouth.

"It's Formosa Oolong, you know," she went on chattily. "I get it from a charming little shop near Union Square. They carry a fantastic assortment..."

"Adena..."

"And the owner is so accommodating! Of course, he knows I'm a steady customer, so I suppose some of the service I get is based on that. And I do pay a bit more for..."

"Adena!"

"A bit more for some of my favorite blends. But I do believe in the old adage that you get what you pay for. Don't you?"

To her surprise, a red flush appeared under his high, tanned cheekbones. His gray eyes glittered ominously as Holt fully comprehended her flippancy.

"I couldn't agree with you more," he said silkily. "Are you by any chance trying to tell me I'm not offering enough? Be reasonable, Adena. We barely know each other. Although that's not altogether my fault," he added reflectively. "If you hadn't taken offense the other evening we might have saved a little time and a great deal of misunderstanding."

"You'll have to forgive me. I was under something of a strain."

"Adena, stop playing games with me! I came here tonight to straighten everything out. The least you can do is stop taunting me. I've said I'm sorry! Now what the hell are you laughing at?"

"You, naturally. Who else? I wasn't in a mood to truly appreciate the humor of the situation the other evening, but tonight I'm finding it delightful. How many other women have you bought in the past six months, Holt? A half dozen or so? Will I be joining a harem? You do understand that Max would have to be part of the deal. His expenses would have to be covered. And then there's the amount I spend on good tea and food every month. I'm afraid I wouldn't be a cheap addition to your collection…!"

"Damn it, woman! I came here with the intention of making you an honest offer of employment and…"

"And a straightforward proposition," she reminded him smoothly.

"That's not it at all!"

"What would you call it?" she inquired interestedly.

He drew a deep breath, obviously making a valiant attempt to hang on to his temper. "I'm sorry if my approach is a little too crude for you. But the simple fact of the matter is I want you, and I'm willing to pay your price."

The directness of his words was too much, even for Adena's sense of humor. It was suddenly her turn to feel the heat rising in her cheeks.

"What makes you so sure you want me?" she managed coolly. "As you said, we've only spent one evening together."

"It was enough," he said, his tone softening and a smile shaping his mouth.

Adena saw the memory of the kiss in his eyes and felt even warmer. The teacup clattered slightly as she placed it back on the saucer. "Where in the world did you get the notion that you could put a price on love, Holt Sinclair?"

"There is a price on everything, Adena. But as it happens, I'm not buying love."

"You're hiring a new housekeeper?" she mocked, abruptly incensed. "Or am I to be a fourth for bridge when you need one? Or perhaps you need a private accountant?"

"I shall be happy to demonstrate the role I expect you to play in my life," he drawled evenly.

Adena had the distinct impression he was beginning to feel more than a little provoked. Which was entirely fair, she told herself spiritedly. He deserved it.

"Thanks, but no thanks, Holt. While it's true that I am looking for another job at the moment, I have no intention of accepting your offer. Too many strings attached, I'm afraid."

"You're angry."

"You're so perceptive."

"Just because I'm being honest in my approach?" He eyed her as if he'd expected better of her.

"Your approach, to put it as clearly as possible, is unsubtle, unromantic, and uninteresting!"

"Unsubtle, I'll grant you, but uninteresting? That I can guarantee to fix. And as for unromantic, that's nonsense. What could be more romantic than two people who meet and are immediately attracted to each other?" he mocked lightly.

Adena smiled recklessly. "Is that what you think happened? Love at first sight?"

"*Attraction* at first sight," he corrected smoothly. "And don't you dare sit there looking like a shocked Victorian heroine and tell me you didn't feel some of the same things I did the other evening. If you didn't, you wouldn't have stayed for dinner and you wouldn't have gone so soft and weak in my arms when I kissed you.''

"Soft and weak!" Adena flared, stung by the gleam in his gray gaze. "Are you out of your mind? You virtually assaulted me! That wasn't a response you were getting—that was me doing my best to endure an unpleasant moment!"

For a second she thought she'd gone too far. Something very masculine looked out at her from his silvery eyes. But in the next instant Holt was smiling wryly and reaching for the other half of his sandwich.

"This is, I suppose, the point at which I should haul you arrogantly into my arms, pin you beneath me on the sofa, and make passionate love to you until you're incapable of denying me anything I want. Kissing you, in fact, into a breathless state of surrender."

"Holt!" Adena felt herself instinctively withdraw into the depths of her chair. It was a useless little movement engendered by a fear she refused to acknowledge. For a fleeting moment in time Adena knew what it was to feel incredibly vulnerable. And he hadn't moved an inch.

"What's the matter? Wouldn't that be romantic enough for you? And you can't say it lacks interest..."

Adena's turquoise eyes narrowed in resentful suspicion. "You're teasing me."

"A little." He grinned unrepentantly and sipped his tea.

"I suppose it wasn't very nice to tell you that I only endured your kiss," Adena managed with a blatantly false attempt at regretful apology.

"Very unkind. Fortunately for my ego I'm prepared to make allowances in this case."

"Decent of you. What allowance could there possibly be, though? It seems to me that, rude as it may sound, you have to accept the facts."

"I do. And knowing those facts, I'm prepared to forego the swift, unsubtle approach. At least for a while."

"Your generosity overwhelms me. What facts would those be?" Adena demanded waspishly.

"Why, that you're still recovering from the shock of ending your other relationship, of course," he returned almost sympathetically. "You have to pretend to yourself that you resisted my kiss the other evening because you would feel terrible if you admitted to responding to another man so soon after giving Carrigan his walking papers. How did he take the news, anyway? I meant to ask you."

Adena stared at him, silently gritting her teeth at a perception for which she would never have given Holt credit. It was dismaying in the extreme to have him so casually put his finger on a nagging truth. He was right; she'd had no business letting Holt Sinclair talk her into staying for dinner the other night. But that memory didn't make her as edgy as the one he was trying to force on her now: the memory of the stirring of attraction she'd experienced in his arms. And she'd felt that attraction only a few hours after saying good-bye to Jeff!

"I don't think he believes I meant it," Adena answered coolly, remembering Jeff's calm assumption that she would reconsider her rash action.

"If he comes around again you'll have to make it very clear to him, won't you?" There was a faint but definite challenge in the deep, unruffled voice. Even Max's ears twitched at it, although he didn't bother to open his eyes. The dog continued dozing comfortably at Holt's feet.

"I don't see that it should concern you," Adena retorted.

Holt's mouth tightened but his words were filled with assurance. "I'll make sure you don't pine for him."

"Why don't you come back in about six months and see if I've managed to get over him on my own?" she snapped tersely.

"I'm a reasonably patient man, but not that patient!" He held out his cup hopefully. "May I have some more tea?"

"Help yourself," she muttered irritably.

"I could but I enjoy watching you pour it. There's something very pleasant about the sight of a woman like you pouring tea."

"It gives you the impression I know my place?" she quipped, giving up the small battle and reaching for the delicate teapot.

"No," he smiled with a charm that unsettled her. "It's just...pleasant. Feminine and civilized..." He broke off as she filled his cup. "Adena, give me a chance, will you? I won't rush you, I promise."

She looked up at him through her lashes as she put down the teapot, aware of a new and more serious element in the conversation.

"I'm not in the market for an affair at the moment, Holt," she told him carefully. "Or should I just say I'm not *on* the market."

He met her eyes in a long glance of speculation and assessment and then he surprised her by saying softly, "We'll talk about it later. Something tells me it's time to change the conversation."

"Before I get so angry that I sic Max on you?" she mocked.

He bent down and tugged at one of Max's ears, smiling as the dog moved his head obligingly. "No, I mean before you get a cornered feeling and start saying things you'll regret."

"Holt, this is ridiculous. I'm not available for purchase like a box of candy...."

"I know that," he grinned. "There's nothing at all cloying about you! Now about our change of topic..."

"I don't think we have all that much in common to discuss!"

"How about your taste in art?"

"What?" Blankly she followed his gaze to a copy of an impressionist painting on the wall behind her.

"It suits you and it suits this room. All light and color and a kind of gentleness." He glanced around the room again, taking in the graceful furniture and the light-filled colors. "I wonder if you have any idea how alluring it all is for a man like me."

"I didn't design it with you in mind!" she protested with a gathering frown, not liking the way she was reacting to the unusual compliment.

"I know that, but the result is the same, isn't it? The moment I walked in I felt welcomed. As if everything was waiting for me..."

"If you didn't surround yourself with such hard-edged masculine furnishings, you probably wouldn't be so affected by a bit of softness," Adena told him accusingly.

"Is that how you saw my home? All hard-edged and masculine? Fascinating!"

"I know I'm going to regret asking this, but what's so fascinating about it?"

"I'm pleased you had such a strong reaction to my surroundings. It's a start in the right direction. Now, can I help you with these tea things?"

He was already on his feet, lifting the silver-tiered tray and starting toward the kitchen. Helplessly, Adena trailed after him, carrying the cups and saucers.

"Holt, I really think it's time you left," she began determinedly, wondering desperately how she could possibly force him out. "You've said what you came to say and I've given you my answer. Please don't be difficult."

"Here, give me those cups. I'll rinse them out for you. I have a hunch you don't put china like this through a dishwasher, right?"

"Right. You don't have to bother washing them, though. I'll take care of them after you leave."

"Wouldn't think of it. I want to impress you with my domesticity," he chuckled, locating the detergent and running hot water into the sink as if he did it on a routine basis.

"I'm sure your housekeeper must love working for you," Adena grumbled, knowing there wasn't much she could do to drag him away from the sink.

"I'll have to ask her." He dipped a cup into the soap suds, then rinsed it thoroughly. "I never got a chance to ask how you discovered those payoffs,

Adena. Tell me about it. I've always had a certain interest in accounting. It seems a bit like magic at times.''

She glared at him distrustfully, watching as he handled her fine china with great care. But it wasn't long before she succumbed to the easy charm Holt was choosing to lavish on her. And asking her about her work seemed harmless enough.

She was deeply involved in the intricacies of accounting checks and balances by the time he finished doing her dishes. He managed to shepherd her gently back into the living room where he poured sherry from the crystal decanter on the cherry-wood table. It occurred to her that Holt was making himself more than a little at home. But she accepted the small glass of sherry and plunged on to finish her explanation.

"Very interesting," he nodded approvingly. "There's nothing like a combination of brains and softness in a woman. Irresistible!"

"I don't know where you get the idea I'm soft!"

"I got it the moment I walked through my study door and found you waiting for me with such an anxious look in those lovely blue-green eyes," he murmured deeply, sitting down across from her. "I told myself that whatever it was you were selling, I'd be buying!"

Adena shook her head wonderingly. "Have you

always seen the world in terms of a commercial transaction?''

He shrugged philosophically. "I'm a practical man.''

"Where did you learn this great practicality?'' In spite of herself, Adena felt a new curiosity about him. How did a man become so thoroughly mercenary?

"In a variety of schools,'' he drawled slowly. Some of the directness disappeared from his gaze as he eyed her. It was as if her question had triggered a hidden shutter.

"Tell me,'' she urged quietly, knowing she shouldn't be pushing the point yet suddenly unable to resist doing exactly that.

He sipped his sherry, regarding her silently for a moment. "I guess you could say I learned it in places like the small farming town where I grew up. The only ticket out was an education or the army. I chose the army because on the surface it seemed less expensive. I was wrong, of course. The army got me out of town, all right, it took me all the way to Southeast Asia where I learned that anything and everything could be bought and sold, including human lives. But I survived mentally and physically, which was a victory of sorts....''

"Go on,'' she urged softly when he allowed the sentence to trail off

"When I got back I bought the education I should have had the sense to buy earlier. I also made another, somewhat unwise, purchase. I bought a wife."

"A wife!"

"Ummm." Holt nodded with a wry twist of his mouth. 'But at the time I didn't fully comprehend the fact that a wife is an installment plan purchase, and a man has to keep up the payments through good times and bad. During one of the downturns in the aerospace industry she found someone who could make the payments in a much grander style than I was managing to do."

"She left you?"

"Like a shot," Holt said with a wry cheerfulness that made Adena wince. "And I can't say that I blame her. In the long run, however, it was all for the best. During the extended layoff I decided I didn't like being at the mercy of a corporate body of strangers. The independence and control over my own life that I wanted could never be achieved working for someone else. So I went into business for myself."

"And the rest," Adena murmured dryly, "is history. You are now able to afford just about anything you desire, right?"

"Just about," he agreed meaningfully.

"I take it you don't see yourself as overly cynical, merely practical?"

"Do you think I'm too cynical?" he returned musingly, as if the notion were a new one.

"Very definitely!"

"That's because you view life through a romantic haze. Like that impressionist painting on your wall. You prefer the light and the cheerful colors."

"Perhaps," she agreed quietly, thinking there might be an element of truth in what he said. She had wanted the man in her life to be shocked at the discovery in Carrigan Labs' accounts. She had wanted Jeff to measure up to some ideal she had in her head about how a man should conduct his business and his life. Perhaps that was impractical.

"It's all right, Adena," Holt growled huskily, setting down his sherry glass. "I can afford your illusions. Tell me what you want and I'll give it to you."

"You think it's all so simple, don't you?" she whispered.

"Try me. Name something you want and I'll tell you whether or not I can give it to you," he challenged gently.

"How about a little business integrity?" she goaded. "How about conducting your business affairs without making payoffs and without industrial espionage?"

He smiled with grim satisfaction and leaned back against the white cushion of the sofa. His gray eyes gleamed at her from under slightly lowered lids.

"I have never," he declared calmly, "made a payoff or taken a kickback in my entire career."

"I don't believe you!" she snapped. "You weren't at all surprised to find out someone on your staff was being paid off! You acted as though it were a routine matter engaged in by all companies!"

"It's not particularly uncommon but that doesn't mean I resort to it. I'm practical enough not to be shocked by it when it occurs, however."

"And you certainly didn't hesitate to offer me a bribe!" she reminded him haughtily.

"That was different."

"How?" she taunted.

"Because I intended to buy you, not your information. I was looking for the fastest and simplest way of securing you; and since I assumed you'd come to sell me the information in the first place, it seemed reasonable also to assume you were approachable from that angle. I never intended to buy genuine secrets about Carrigan Labs from you."

"You expect me to believe that?"

"The fact that I'm still trying to buy you even though you've quit your job should tell you something. Besides," Holt said with a teasing smile, "if I were really intent on obtaining solid industrial secrets from Carrigan Labs, I would have approached someone a little higher up than yourself. Okay, that's one illusion which can be maintained intact. I'm honest in my business dealings. What's next on your list?''

"I'm not going down a shopping list and checking off my requirements," Adena announced aloofly. "Something tells me you'd have an answer for anything!"

"Probably."

"You're so damned cynical!" she exclaimed, at the end of her patience.

There was a pause before he suggested very quietly, "So change me."

Adena caught her breath at the outrageous remark. "Are you out of your mind?"

"No, but I do try to keep it open. I think my approach to life is entirely pragmatic, but I'm willing to let you try to change my mind."

"You're trying to manipulate me!" she gritted, beating down the sense of intrigue he'd aroused with his dare.

"Now you're the one who's being cynical," he smiled lazily.

"There's a difference between cynicism and caution."

He leaned forward intently, one elbow braced on his knee, his chin resting on the heel of his palm.

His gray eyes swept her with a silent, urgent message that was difficult to ignore. "Have dinner with me tomorrow evening, Adena, I promise not to assault you in the restaurant or afterward. I may be cynical but I can behave like a gentleman on the few occasions in life when it's necessary."

"And you've decided tomorrow night it might be necessary?" she asked whimsically, thinking that she shouldn't even be considering the suggestion and knowing it was already starting to tantalize her.

"I'm willing to cater to your taste for romantic illusions to the extent of making a few of them real."

"You think that's my price?"

"I think you won't be able to resist the idea of trying to make a dent in my cynicism," he retorted. "I'm offering you an evening with no strings attached. Just a pleasant evening for two. How about it?"

Adena bit her lip, astounded at herself for even contemplating accepting the invitation. Before she could make up her mind to refuse outright, Holt stretched out a hand and captured her wrist.

"Please, Adena?" he begged in that deep voice that threatened to drag her under. "I give you my word: no strings. Just let me take you out on a proper date."

"And afterward?" she got out throatily as he stood up and pulled her to her feet beside him.

"And afterward I'll bring you home and leave you on your doorstep if that's what you want."

Adena felt the warmth of him through the weave of his sweater. He continued to hold her wrist in a gentle grip, but he didn't really force the kiss on her lips. She simply found herself standing acquiescently when he bent his head and lightly touched her mouth with his own.

When he withdrew a few inches, Adena lowered her lashes, deeply aware of the knowledge that she wanted more. One date. What harm could there be in one date if he gave her his word he would take her home afterward without any argument?

"Don't be afraid of me, Adena. I admit I want you, but I'm willing to play the game your way. I'm not a twenty-year-old boy who's out for only one thing."

"Aren't you?" she insisted a little breathlessly. She was standing too near the fire in him, she realized vaguely. She ought to put some distance between them. As it was, the masculine aura surrounding him threatened to override her judgment. She sensed the physical strength that could spell either reassurance and protection for a woman—or danger. Adena also knew the impact of a more subtle power—that of an iron will. It reached out to surround her silently and draw her closer.

"No," he denied on a flickering note of humor. "I'm thirty-eight and capable of appreciating more than one aspect of a relationship. Take a chance, honey. I can make you forget Carrigan and I can behave like a gentleman."

"And if you don't wind up getting what you want?"

"I'll take the risk."

"Because you don't expect to fail," she concluded for him.

"I'll take the risk," he repeated deliberately, "because an evening out with you on a real date will be worth a lot in itself."

Adena told herself she shouldn't let the blatant flattery coax her into a potentially dangerous situation, but she was weakening and she knew it.

Heaven help her! She wanted to go out with him! She wanted it so badly that she was willing to believe all his fine promises.

"All right, Holt," she said slowly, as if testing the water at the edge of the sea. She would have to be careful how far out she waded, but surely she could handle a short distance?

"Thank you," he said on a groan that ended against her lips.

This time the kiss was more than a feathery brush, but it didn't threaten. Gently, persuasively, Holt deepened the electrical contact between them until Adena began to relax against his body. He was so strong, so warm; it was a temptation to lean against him and let him hold her more completely.

She hadn't realized just how far she had swum from the safety of the shore, though, until Holt abruptly broke off the kiss to bury his lips in the umber softness of her hair. His hand slid slowly up the length of her spine beneath her green tunic and he strung a chain of light, fiercely restrained kisses down the curve of her throat and onto the portion of her shoulder bared by the bateau neckline. Adena shivered and she knew he felt it.

As if she were wrenching herself free of entangling seaweed, she stepped back. He let her go readily enough, his hands falling away from her without protest.

"I'll pick you up at seven," he promised, turning away to find his jacket. Adena thought she saw a flash of pure satisfaction in his smoky gray eyes, but it was gone when he faced her once again. "If you get cold feet between now and tomorrow evening, just tell yourself I owe you a night on the town," he chuckled. "Since you don't feel you can accept the offer of employment, it's the least I can do!"

Then he was gone, leaving Max wagging his tail at the door and Adena with a feeling that some vital component of her charming room had suddenly vanished.

Four

Holt picked her up the next evening in a gunmetal gray Ferrari that proved a perfect backdrop for the ebony and gold-brushed metallic print dress Adena had chosen with unusual care. His eyes flickered with undisguised pleasure as he absorbed the picture she made in the full-sleeved gown with its wide gold belt and low neckline.

"You look very lovely tonight," he murmured deeply as he took her arm. The gold and black sleeve of her dress brushed against the fine material of the dark, subtly striped European suit he was wearing. Adena had the impression Holt liked that touch of familiarity.

"I always try to make a good impression on the first date," Adena said lightly. The lightness in her voice was as much a defense against the controlled hunger in his gray gaze as it was against her own reaction to his attraction for her. The sable darkness of his hair was carefully combed; she found herself longing to muss it with her fingertips.

"Thank you," he murmured, closing the door politely on Max's hopeful face and leading Adena out to the Ferrari.

"For making a good impression?"

"For treating this as a first date." He slid into the seat beside her and gave Adena a searching glance. "I meant what I said, honey, we'll do this your way."

"You mean you'll give me what I want?" she teased softly. "Pay my price by behaving like a gentleman?"

A slow, slashing grin crossed his mouth as he turned the key in the ignition. "I can afford it. For a while."

The Ferrari surged with restrained power across the Golden Gate Bridge. A short distance north Holt took the Alexander turnoff and began the descent to Bridgeway, the waterfront main street of Sausalito. The stair-stepped houses rose above them as they followed the winding road.

The boutique-lined street along the water's edge

was also the location of several chic restaurants, and
Adena wasn't surprised when Holt chose one of the
best.

"You know how to make a good impression
yourself," Adena remarked as the shrimp cocktail
adorned with basil arrived sometime later at the can-
dlelit table. "Be aware, however, that I don't gen-
erally allow my dates to order for me."

"I appreciate the fact that you were willing to
place yourself in my hands tonight," he drawled.
"Next time I promise to ask your preferences."

"Would you allow me to indulge them if you
thought there was something more interesting on the
menu?"

"You seem to have formed the notion that I'm
the domineering type," he chuckled, watching her
nibble at the basil shrimp.

"I think you have a definite tendency in that direction," she agreed half seriously. "You would
need to be properly handled in a long-term relationship or you'd take over completely."

Holt's mouth lifted in amusement as he swirled
the Chenin Blanc in his wine glass. Across the expanse of glowing white table cloth and polished silver his gray eyes met her turquoise ones and neither
looked away.

"I like to think I'm adaptable," he declared modestly.

"Everyone likes to think that but most of us aren't. People who are accustomed to getting their own way are probably the least adaptable because they've had the least amount of experience in adapting!"

"Is there a message in all this for me?" he murmured interestedly.

"Think of it as a warning," she advised with humorous daring.

Holt looked down at the pale gold wine in his glass and asked softly, "Are you afraid of me?"

"Of course not. If I were afraid of you I wouldn't have accepted your invitation this evening!" Was that the truth?

"But you're determined to keep me in my place tonight?" he pressed softly.

"Definitely," Adena confirmed cheerfully. And she did feel very much in control this evening, she thought wonderingly. Or was that really a feeling of recklessness? Was there a difference?

"You already have my word that I'll behave myself," he pointed out blandly. "So are you certain it's me you're determined to control?"

"Surely you're not going to suggest that I find myself in danger of going crazy with desire tonight?" she taunted.

"It's a pleasant thought," he sighed wistfully.

Adena laughed, her eyes gleaming with the

amusement and excitement racing through her veins. She felt a little high and she hadn't even finished one glass of wine. The electricity in the air was a tangible thing tonight, affecting her more than she would have believed possible.

"Do you spend all your non-working hours encouraging women to make fools of themselves over you?" she demanded.

He considered the question. "No. Believe it or not I do have other interests in life."

"Such as?"

"They're not very exciting," he cautioned.

"I'm listening."

"Well, I like to go fishing up in the mountains when I get the chance."

"A proper, masculine sort of hobby," Adena approved.

"And I sometimes enjoy painting," he concluded tentatively.

"Painting?" Adena considered that. "What sort of painting?"

"Watercolors."

"Watercolors!" she exclaimed, taken by surprise. "*You* like to do soft, delicate watercolors?"

"You don't have to act quite so stunned by the revelation," he complained mildly.

She ignored his protest. "But where are they? I didn't see any hanging in your home."

"They don't exactly fit the déecor," he conceded wryly. "They usually wind up getting tossed out. I'm not very good at it, you see," he added with a self-deprecating grin. "In fact, I'm quite terrible. But sometimes it suits my mood to get out the paints and experiment."

"I never would have guessed," she smiled, shaking her head.

His small confession seemed to set a tone of intimacy and warmth for the remainder of the evening. It was as if by having revealed a softer side of his nature, Holt had made it possible for both of them to do more than verbally spar and banter. Adena didn't waste the opportunity. She wanted to know more and more about this man.

"Are you always so full of questions on a first date?" he teased affectionately a long time later as she went into his arms on the dance floor.

"You don't like chatty women?"

"I'm just not accustomed to someone wanting to know quite so many details. Tomorrow night it's my turn to ask the questions."

"Is that your subtle way of inviting me out again tomorrow evening?" Adena asked, lifting her head to smile up at him from beneath her lashes. The flirtation was not deliberate but it had the effect of causing Holt to draw her more firmly into his arms. Adena didn't protest.

"Will Max let you go out two nights in a row?"

"We'll have to ask him. He doesn't approve of late hours."

Indeed, it was a somewhat disapproving and sleepy dog who greeted them two hours later when Holt finally took Adena home. Max made certain both were safe and sound and then he flopped down behind the couch on the persimmon rug and went back to sleep, his duty done.

"What a grouch," Holt whispered as he poured himself a sherry and sank lazily down on the couch. "Is he always this way late at night?"

Adena, who had watched the familiar manner in which Holt had helped himself to the sherry, hastily excused her dog. "I warned you."

"Well, it's nice to know you have someone here to look after you when I'm not around," Holt decided philosophically, propping his feet on the coffee table.

"Schnauzers are very loyal and protective," Adena told him as she sat down on the sofa beside Holt. Unobtrusively she managed to leave a discreet space between them.

"Excellent qualities in man or beast," he opined.

"I couldn't agree more," Adena retorted meaningfully. When Holt shot her a reproachful glance, she covered her momentary embarrassment by a sip out of his sherry glass.

"I can be very loyal and protective," he murmured huskily as he leaned back and idly lifted a hand to thrust it beneath the curve of her hair. "Also resourceful, clever, playful and gener—"

"Don't say it or I'll ask you to leave before you've even finished the sherry!"

"Why are you so wary of my generosity?" he grated deeply, turning his head far enough to drop a tiny, tingling kiss on her throat.

"I have the feeling your gifts would come with far too many strings attached," she whispered very seriously, not looking at him.

"And you want your freedom?"

"I just don't want you to feel cheated, which is what would happen if I were to accept your gifts and then didn't give you everything you expected in return!" she told him briskly, trying to break the magic spell which she had allowed to weave itself around her during the evening.

"It's true, I wouldn't take kindly to being cheated. I would expect full value...." Holt was leaning close again, his lips grazing the sensitive skin behind her ear as he lifted her hair aside.

When Adena stirred, instinct telling her it was time to set some boundaries, he caught her chin in the palm of his hand and tilted her face upward for his kiss.

"Adena..."

She shivered as he slowly, inevitably, deepened the caress, once more invading her mouth in a warm, damp kiss of lazy passion.

It was the outward laziness which lulled her normal caution, Adena realized, even as she felt herself on the brink of succumbing to the moment. There was no hint of genuine danger because Holt seemed entirely in control of himself. She could relax for a little while and enjoy the trembling excitement he created in her. And what harm could there be in a good-night kiss?

With a moan that seemed to catch in her throat, Adena lifted her fingertips to the pelt of near-black hair which almost demanded to be disarranged. Tentatively she thrust gilded nails into the dark depths and was instantly rewarded with a tautening in his hard body that thrilled her.

Her senses ignited at the evidence of his response. When her fingers tightened in his hair, Holt cradled her against his arm, forcing her head gently down on his shoulder.

"Adena, my sweet, let me warm myself at your fire tonight. You feel so delightful in my arms and I want you so badly…!"

Holt slid a questing, probing hand along the outer edge of her thigh up to her waist. The material of her ebony and gold dress provided little protection against the enticing feel of his fingers as they stroked upward. Adena trembled and nestled closer, her lashes flickering against her cheek as she closed her eyes to the risks she was taking.

When his thumb moved slowly, encouragingly to the tip of her breast, Adena sucked in her breath. She had worn no bra under the silky material of the dress and he found her small, rounded softness with a muttered exclamation of male desire.

She turned her head against his neck, her lips parting in a soft sigh. When his fingers began to move more demandingly on her tautening nipple, she found herself clinging to him with an abandon that should have astounded her, but seemed entirely natural at that moment. Unthinkingly she arched closer.

"Holt...oh, Holt...!"

"What's the matter, sweetheart?" he whispered in husky amusement as the passion in her communicated itself to him. "Don't you like what we're doing to each other?"

"It's...it's too soon..." she began helplessly, just as his hand moved from her breast to the fastening of her dress. The material seemed to fall away, baring her to the waist before she could summon a coherent protest.

"It's not too soon, honey," he rasped, bending his head to taste the upper slope of one breast. "It wouldn't have been too soon that first night. I was meant to have you for my own. I knew it the moment I saw you!''

Adena cried out softly as he shifted position, pressing her down onto the cushions beneath him. Her black, strappy evening sandals slipped off her feet to fall unnoticed on the persimmon rug.

''Trust me, darling,'' he soothed, letting meltingly hot kisses rain down her throat to her swelling breasts. ''I'll take care of you. I'll take care of everything.''

It was such a temptation to take him at his word—to trust him. A distant voice in Adena's mind shouted an even more distant warning. This was the man who thought he could buy anyone or anything. He didn't understand the emotions of love, he only knew he wanted her. How could she be contemplating surrender to Holt Sinclair?

'I trust you, Holt,'' she managed, her fingers splaying across his shoulders under his suit jacket. ''I trust you to know what you want. It's myself I'm unsure of....''

''Let me stay with you tonight. You'll be sure of everything by morning,'' he vowed, shrugging out of the jacket. As he hovered briefly above her his gray eyes flared with hungry intent. A lambent silver flame seemed to burn in them, showering sparks over her bare skin. Before Adena could find the words to protest, he was crushing her back into the cushions, his tie and jacket left in a careless heap on the floor.

Burying his face in her throat, he wrapped her in a passionate embrace. His lower body sank heavily against hers, awakening her to the desire building in him. His implicit demand seemed to pull at her senses, forcing thoughts of protest further back in her mind. She was discovering that for her there was an unbelievable allure in this man. An allure that threatened to swamp all her normal reasoning processes.

When her fingers went shakily to the buttons of his crisp white shirt, Holt groaned with a deep pleasure that was a reward in itself. There was something very satisfying about being able to arouse this particular man, Adena realized.

The white shirtfront parted, revealing an expanse of tanned, sleekly muscled chest. The curling hair which tapered down to his waist was a new enticement to her kneading fingertips, and her gilded nails once again sank into a dark cloud.

"My God! Adena, I want you so badly...!"

His deep, undersea voice washed across her senses in a wave that left her clinging. Without consciously willing it, she arched her hips upward, seeking the promise of his warmth, and when he felt the feminine plea, Holt let his hand glide down her side to her hip, pushing her ebony and gold dress farther aside. Then he lifted himself for a moment and removed her dress completely.

"Let me show you how good it's going to be, sweetheart," he commanded warmly as he stared down into her widened turquoise eyes. "You won't regret anything, I swear."

"Holt, you're rushing me," she got out shakily, feeling helpless to stop the flood. "You promised you wouldn't rush me...."

The soft light in the room poured over her nearly nude body, illuminating the satiny triangle of lace which was all that remained to cover her, and the necklace of gold dragonfly wings that still circled her throat. It was to the jewelry rather than to her delicate underwear that Holt's fingers moved almost convulsively.

"This makes you look like a captured slave girl, did you know that? Very erotic." He smiled a little dangerously and traced the shape of the golden wings with his lips. When Adena moved beneath him he slid his hand down to the curve of her hip but didn't raise his head.

"Admit you want me, sweet slave girl," he growled against her skin. "Give me that much, at least!"

She wound her arms around his body beneath his open shirt, her breath coming quickly between her lips as he clenched her buttocks in deep arousal.

"You must...you must know I want you," she gasped, her head falling back beneath his burning kisses.

"I want to hear you say it," he urged thickly.

Once again recklessness took hold. "What will you give me if I say it?" she whispered on a note of daring, taunting laughter.

There was a sudden, unexpected stillness in him which startled her. But before she could orient her whirling senses sufficiently to question the change in his mood, it was gone. Instead, the hand on her hip tightened almost painfully, and he sank his teeth into the flesh of her shoulder in a small nip that made her flinch. His entire body felt like a tightly coiled spring against her softness.

"Anything you want," he promised with the rashness of a man totally caught up in the passion of the moment. "Ask for anything you want and if it's in my power, I'll give it to you. Just let me hear you say you want me!"

"There is nothing you can give me that will make me say it, Holt Sinclair," she told him huskily, her blue-green eyes darkening with the depths of her emotions. "Nothing at all!"

He raised his head to stare tightly down at her, the taut line of his cheekbones and the lines at the edge of his mouth giving his expression a hard, ravaged look that tore at her senses.

"Adena!"

Instantly she softened, her taunting, teasing reck-lessness giving way at once to the need to comfort. Running her fingers lightly through his hair, she looked up at him with deep emotion.

"I said there was nothing you could give me that would make me say the words, Holt, and I meant it. But I will say them for free: I want you. I have never wanted a man as badly as I want you tonight."

The heat of his gaze was scorching. For an instant she thought he would speak but then, as if he were at a loss for words, Holt lowered himself to her once more, inhaling the fragrance of her hair. She felt the tense need in him and gently, lovingly stroked his back.

Lovingly, Adena thought silently, turning the word over in her mind. It seemed to fit very nicely. Was she falling in love with Holt Sinclair? Was that why her common sense and her normally control-lable emotions had deserted her tonight?

The thought frightened her as nothing else could have at that moment. It jolted her back to reality, making her horribly conscious of her nudity, and of the intimacy of the situation.

"Adena, what's wrong? Don't freeze up on me! Not now, not tonight! I want to make you mine com-pletely. I must!"

That pleading command was almost her undoing.

Only the fear of being on the brink of a very dangerous emotion kept Adena from slipping over the edge and into the depths of the sea. She needed time. She had to think. And it was all happening so fast…!

"Please, Holt," she begged. "Please, you said you wouldn't rush me. I need time.…"

"Adena, I want you and you want me. You've admitted that much. Can't you trust me tonight?"

"It's too soon…" She breathed the words almost sadly, knowing they were true but wishing they weren't.

He lay heavily along the length of her, holding her immobile and letting her feel the strength in him. He didn't need to point out the obvious. They both knew he could take her and in the end she would give herself willingly. Their eyes met in mutual recognition of that salient fact and Adena waited for Holt's decision.

For a moment the electric tension flowing between them was so thick Adena thought she could see it. Then, with a growling exclamation of resignation that said more clearly than words how reluctant Holt was to accede to her wishes, he sat up beside her on the sofa.

She lay there, feeling bereft, and watched the play of emotions across his rugged face.

"Thank you, Holt," she said gently.

"For acting the gentleman tonight? Don't thank me. I feel like a world-class fool!"

He surged to his feet, his eyes raking her nudity until she shivered again. He had a way of making her feel so incredibly vulnerable! Hastily Adena reached for the froth of ebony and gold and stepped into the dress as Holt buttoned his shirt. His brooding gaze never left her figure, and it sent the blood rushing into her cheeks as she dressed.

They stood looking at each other in silence as they finished adjusting their clothing. Finally Holt stepped forward with a swift, convulsive movement, pulling her tightly into his arms.

"Tomorrow night," he gritted tightly. "Be ready around six, all right?"

"Okay." Adena knew she couldn't have refused.

His hold on her tightened and he kissed the heaviness of her hair. "Adena, I don't want to go home tonight."

"I know," she whispered achingly.

"But you're going to send me home, anyway?" he concluded with wry humor that broke the tension a little. "Why is Max looking at me like that?" he added a little aggressively.

Adena turned her head to follow his gaze. Max was peeking around the edge of the sofa, his chin resting on his paws. "He's waiting to escort you politely to the door."

"I know when I'm licked," Holt groaned, dropping a last, hard kiss on her upturned mouth before reaching down to scoop up his jacket.

At the door he stopped, his hand on the knob. "Don't forget, tomorrow night."

"How could I forget?"

"We'll go to Chinatown…!"

"How about dinner here, instead?" She hadn't meant to make the offer but somehow it slipped out before she could think. She wanted him in her home, wanted him lending his solid, dark presence to the light, graceful apartment.

"I'll bring the wine," he offered at once, as if afraid she might back out if he gave her a chance to think.

She nodded.

"Good night, Adena."

"Good night, Holt."

The door closed firmly behind him, leaving Max and Adena alone. As if both were momentarily entranced, dog and woman continued staring silently at the closed door.

"He thinks he can buy me, Max."

The dog lifted his muzzle inquiringly, coming toward her as if to offer comfort and security. She reached down and scratched his ears affectionately. "I have to teach him that some things can't be bought, dog. Some things have to be given freely. Do you think he's capable of learning that lesson?''

Max's dark eyes peered earnestly up at her through a long fringe of silvery lashes.

"You like him, don't you?" Adena smiled. "Something tells me you've already made your decision. It's probably just that you're so happy to see Jeff gone!''

It was strange how the initial uneasiness she had experienced over being able to respond to another man so soon after breaking off the relationship with Jeff had disappeared. Jeff had been all wrong for her, Adena told herself as she trailed bemusedly through the apartment, turning off lights. Perhaps she had known that deep down. Perhaps that was what had made it so simple to break up with Jeff over a business issue like the payoffs. Would she be able to walk away from a man like Holt so easily if she were to discover that he didn't meet her standards of integrity?

But that was a ridiculous notion, Adena scolded herself as she undressed and slipped into a champagne-colored nightgown. She'd only spent three evenings with the man and the first couple could hardly be described as totally amicable!

There was no denying they had learned a great deal about each other during those evenings, though. Adena's mouth tightened ruefully. And she certainly had learned enough to know Holt Sinclair wasn't the sort of man with whom she should be getting involved. Unless…unless he could learn to love eventually; learn to trust in another's love…learn that one didn't buy a relationship with another human being—at least not a real and lasting relationship!

It wouldn't surprise her to find out Holt had quite successfully bought several relationships in the past. Did he realize they were the wrong kind? Could he be made to realize that fact?

Adena snuggled into the pillow, analyzing the evening, thinking of the conversation which had run the gamut from teasing banter to a serious discussion of where she had sent her résumés.

That reminded her, she'd better think about following up on a few of those job inquiries. One didn't get a good position without a great deal of proper groundwork. She didn't want to have to take just anything that came along.

Briefly she remembered her earlier thoughts of taking a small vacation and heading toward the gold country of the Sierra Nevada Mountains. Somehow that idea didn't beckon as strongly as it had at first. She wasn't certain what she had with Holt Sinclair, but she knew now she didn't want to abandon it. Not yet.

With a deep yawn, Max padded softly into the

bedroom and settled down on the carpet at the foot of the bed. Adena smiled to herself.

"I hope you know what I'm doing, Max, because I'm not at all certain that *I* do!"

Max stirred comfortably but gave no other response. Adena knew him well enough to know his very lack of concern was answer enough. She remembered how the dog had growled at Jeff every time he had come to the apartment, and she wondered how Max had known from the beginning that Jeff Carrigan wasn't good husband material.

"Not that Holt is, either," Adena added aloud to the silent dog. "He doesn't even understand about love yet. You can bet marriage isn't at the top of his list of most-wanted-items for Christmas!"

Which brought up the uncomfortable notion of what it would be like to have an affair with him. Adena had the impression it would be an all or nothing relationship Holt would eventually demand. She suspected he was being relatively patient with her now but sooner or later he would want everything from her.

What would she do when that time came? Not wanting to think about it, Adena buried her face in the pillow and added up columns of imaginary numbers in her head until she fell asleep.

Five

Adena was putting the finishing touches on the Belgian endive, beet, and avocado salad the next evening when the doorbell sounded. Holt was early, she thought in amusement, wiping her fingers daintily on a tea towel and heading toward the door.

She moved gracefully in a wine velvet skirt which she had paired with a romantic, high-necked, long-sleeved blouse trimmed in ruffles and lace and buckled with a smashing Mexican silver and turquoise belt. Congratulating herself that she had started dinner preparations a bit early, Adena rounded the corner of the kitchen door to find that Max had already reached the front door ahead of her.

It was the schnauzer's distinctly forbidding air which told Adena that whoever stood outside her door, it wasn't Holt. Her eyebrows drew together in a troubled frown as she depressed the intercom button.

"Who is it?"

The shock she experienced when Jeff Carrigan's voice came back over the speaker told Adena just how far out of her mind she had managed to put the man who had once been so important to her.

"Open up, Adena. We have a little matter to discuss."

"Jeff! What in the world!"

Reluctantly she opened the door, intending to send the man on his way, but before she could say anything, he pushed into the apartment, crowding her back.

In an instant she realized he was furiously angry. His handsome features were twisted into an angry threat and she was almost certain he'd had a few drinks.

"Jut what the hell kind of game do you think you're playing, Adena West," he raged tightly, coming toward her.

"Jeff, calm down," she snapped, surprised at his show of temper. She wouldn't have given him credit for such depth of emotion. "What's the matter with you? And stop yelling at me. The neighbors will hear!''

''I don't give a damn who hears! Did you think I'd let you get away with a cheap trick like this? You little bitch! I'm going to wring your neck!''

A warning growl interrupted the furious monologue. Max was standing stiff-legged with aggression. He watched the intruder with the inborn hostility of a dog whose ancestors had been used for centuries as guard dogs.

''Max! Down!'' Adena said sharply, sensing that in another instant the dog would be leaping for any part of Jeff he thought he could reach. Max obeyed to the point of not springing at the man, but he didn't back away. Another low growl sounded dangerously far back in his throat.

''Call off your damn dog, Adena! He's not going to do you much good anyway!''

''Jeff, stop raging at me and tell me what's going on! Why are you behaving like an animal yourself? We have nothing left between us and you know it. I told you so the day I came to you about those payoffs!''

''And took off to find Sinclair so you could peddle your information to him!''

''That's not true!'' Stricken, Adena drew back a step. ''I...I gave you a chance to stop those payoffs, and when you made it clear you weren't going to do any such thing, I felt an obligation to inform SinTech of what was going on! But I didn't sell the information, I only did what I thought was right under the circumstances!''

Jeff closed in on her and Adena experienced a flicker of genuine fear. If things got worse she was going to have to scream for help. What did Jeff think he was doing, anyway?

"Don't bother lying to me! I know you sold yourself and the information both to the bastard! You were out with him last night down in Sausalito!''

"How did you know about that?'' Adena stared up at his enraged face.

"You were seen,'' he snarled. ''And don't think the person who saw you hesitated to bring the little matter to my attention today. What other information have you sold, Adena? What other Carrigan secrets have you traded for the honor of being Holt Sinclair's latest mistress?''

"I didn't sell information, damn it! I told him the truth about the payoffs because I felt he had a right to know, but I didn't *sell* him the news! It wouldn't have done me any good if I'd tried, you fool, because he already knew who was giving you SinTech data!''

"The hell he did! Our man was providing us with information right up until the day after you walked out!''

"If it's stopped it's only because Holt put an end to it. He said he was only waiting until he had sufficient evidence."

"No wonder you didn't plan to come back to your job! You knew you'd burned your bridges in favor of a better offer from Sinclair, didn't you! But it's not going to work, Adena! I'll teach you to walk out on me and sell yourself to a higher bidder! I'll bet he's not fool enough to offer marriage, though. Better take what you can get in the way of pretty little trinkets, because Sinclair doesn't make a habit of marrying his women!"

"Jeff!"

Adena's voice rose in sudden dismay as he reached for her. She heard Max's growl deepen ominously as she turned to escape. Jeff ignored the dog, clearly not seeing much danger in the animal, or perhaps still too enraged with Adena to pay heed.

Adena's attempt to evade him failed. With a lunge Carrigan grabbed for her wrist, yanking her off balance.

"No!"

The single protest from Adena was all that was finally needed to send Max into action. He lunged for Carrigan's leg just as the front door swung open with a crash.

"What the hell...?"

Adena heard Holt's icy voice as he came swiftly

through the door. But she didn't really see him as she struggled to escape Carrigan's grasp.

In that last effort she was assisted by Max. She heard her captor yell and knew the dog had sunk his teeth into Jeff's leg. The hold on her wrist slackened, and in the next second Jeff Carrigan was being whirled away from her.

"Take your hands off her, or I'll pull you apart, piece by piece!"

Max was barking now, short, snarling yelps of encouragement for Holt, who had flung his victim away from Adena and toward the front door.

"She's mine," Holt rasped as Jeff landed against the door frame. "And if you so much as touch her again I'll not only destroy you, I'll destroy Carrigan Labs. Do you understand me, Carrigan? What I have, I protect, and it will cost you everything if you ever forget that fact!"

"You're welcome to her, Sinclair," Jeff grated, edging through the door. His face was still reddened with the force of his rage, but common sense took hold as he realized the situation in which he found himself. One didn't get to be a vice-president at Carrigan Labs without some native intelligence, even if one was the president's son. "She's obviously a cheap little tramp out for what she can get, and if that's your style in women, help yourself. Personally, I'm glad I found out in time before I made the mistake of marrying her!''

''Get out of here, Carrigan!''

Max issued another warning bark, advancing to stand beside Holt. Together, they made a formidable pair, Adena thought a little hysterically. Apparently Jeff Carrigan came to the same conclusion. He jerked himself away from the door and down the short flight of steps to the street.

Without waiting to see the other man out of sight, Holt slammed the door shut with a decisive movement which seemed to satisfy Max.

The dog turned at once and trotted back to Adena who was shakily leaning on a cherry-wood bookcase. She looked from the dog's proud muzzle to the face of the man behind him and groaned aloud as she thought she detected a similarity in their expressions.

''If you two are looking for medals,'' she began wryly, ''don't expect anything from me! I detest scenes!'' Then, as delayed relief flooded over her, she dropped to her knees and cradled the dog's head in her arms. ''Oh, Max...Max. Where on earth did you learn such ungentlemanly behavior?''

''It comes naturally to the male of the species,'' Holt informed her harshly, dropping down on one knee beside her and pulling her with rough urgency into his arms. ''My God, Adena! When I came through that door and saw him attacking you I wanted to kill him! What the hell happened? What was Carrigan doing here?''

Still trembling in the aftermath of the scene, Adena buried her face in the suede of his jacket and exhaled a long sigh of relief. The feel of his arms around her and the solid hardness of his chest were vastly steadying factors in a world which had gone crazy for a few seconds.

''He…he found out I was seeing you. He thought I'd sold the information about the SinTech informant to you and that I was selling you other Carrigan secrets as well. And he…and he accused me of…'' Adena broke off, unable to repeat all of Jeff's accusations.

''Accused you of what, Adena?'' Holt probed gently, his hands moving soothingly on her spine.

''Never mind,'' she murmured, lifting her head away with a determined, if slightly tremulous, smile. ''He'd had a few drinks, I think. He said several things which are better left unsaid. And even though I hate scenes, I must admit I was very happy to have you come through that door when you did!''

He met her eyes but he didn't return the smile. ''You should never have let him in, Adena.''

''Well, I didn't exactly invite him in,'' she protested, sensing a lecture now that the immediate crisis was over. "I just answered the door with my normal civility and he invited himself inside!"

Holt got to his feet and hauled her up beside him. Max nuzzled Adena's knees, looking for reassurance that she was all right. Somehow, it was easier to deal with Max than Holt's determined expression.

"Yes, Max. You're a good dog! I was very proud of you!" Adena leaned down to pat his gray head approvingly. "But, then, you never did like Jeff, did you? Are you sure you weren't just looking for an excuse to kick him out of the house?"

"Adena, this isn't a joke," Holt bit out, placing a firm hand on each of her shoulders and forcing her back around to face him. "I want your word you won't have any contact with Carrigan again."

"Well," she began briskly, "I don't see that as being much of a problem. I got the distinct impression Jeff doesn't want to see me again, either!"

"I mean it, Adena. You're not to open the door to him, speak to him on the phone, or otherwise allow him near you!"

"Don't worry," she retorted, becoming a little annoyed. "I won't get in touch with him, I promise. I'm quite happy to see the last of him, believe me. Now, if you don't mind, I'd like to call attention to the fact that I'm the innocent victim here. I'd like a little more sympathy and a little less lecturing!"

There was a tense pause while Holt clearly debated whether or not to continue the lecture; then he muttered something unintelligible and hugged her close. "You little idiot. Can't you see Max and I still have all that adrenalin pumping through our systems? It takes a while to revert to a state of normal civility, as you term it, after protecting our private property!"

"Private property!" she yelped. "I like that! What kind of gallantry is that supposed to be? You weren't protecting private property, damn it! You came to the aid of a lady in distress!"

"Whatever you say, honey," he placated, holding her with a fierce possessiveness that belied his words.

"And the lady in distress is quite grateful," Adena continued brightly, pushing herself gently but firmly away from him. She turned a brilliant smile upward. "For Max there will be a lovely bone with lots of juicy meat left on it."

"And for me?" Holt prompted, his gray eyes softening with the first hint of indulgent humor.

"For you a nice home-cooked meal."

"What more could a man ask for?" he sighed, making no secret of his disappointment in her answer.

Adena glanced around hopefully "Did the wine survive?"

"Of course. Did you think I was going to waste

a '79 Chardonnay by breaking it over Carrigan's head?'' he demanded reproachfully, striding across the room to where a bottle waited in a paper sack by the door.

"I'm glad you had the presence of mind to keep your priorities straight," she approved airily, moving toward the kitchen and the unfinished salad dressing.

Holt followed with the Chardonnay and set it down on a tiled counter top. Then with an easy familiarity, he spun around one of the little kitchen table chairs and straddled it backward, resting his elbows on the back as he watched Adena put the finishing touches on dinner.

"Smells delicious," he murmured, eyeing everything with interest.

"Good." She was intensely aware of him, knowing his gray eyes were following her with great intent. Out of the corner of her eye she watched him remove his suede jacket and sling it over a convenient chair. He was wearing a gray cashmere sweater with a finely striped shirt underneath and dark slacks. His sable hair was rakishly tousled from the brief flurry of activity with Jeff. Adena swallowed as she realized how enormously attractive he appeared to her. As she cut the zucchini into narrow julienne strips, Max wandered into the kitchen and flopped down beside Holt's chair.

"Why don't I pour us a little before-dinner sherry?" Holt suggested.

"The last time I saw you helping yourself to my sherry, it was after dinner," Adena reminded him with a smile.

"Sherry is very versatile," he informed her, disappearing briefly and returning with two small crystal glasses full of the golden liquid. He set one down beside her on the counter and resumed his chair.

Adena lifted her glass for a sip. "Will this settle your racing adrenalin?" she teased, setting the glass aside while she went back to slicing zucchini. There was something very homey and pleasant about sharing a drink with Holt while she went about her kitchen duties.

"Nothing like a shot of sherry to deal with raging adrenalin," Holt conceded. "Do you think I ought to give Max some?"

"Liquor," Adena intoned, "has never touched Max's lips!"

"Well, then, it's about time. How old is he, anyway?"

"He's two and a half. Holt! What are you doing?" Adena turned around in time to see Holt calmly pouring a little of his sherry into a saucer for the curious dog.

"You mustn't be overprotective, darling. It's time the lad grew up."

"If you turn my dog into a lush, I swear I'll..."

"Nonsense. Max is a dog of dignity and restraint. See? He knows how to drink sherry."

Adena watched askance as Max delicately lapped at the liquor. Holt was looking so pleased with himself that she had a sudden burst of intuition.

"Holt, have you ever had a pet?"

He looked up, vaguely surprised by the question. "No, come to think of it, I haven't. They weren't allowed at the orphanage and I haven't had time for one since..."

"Orphanage!" Adena stared at him, aghast. "You grew up in an *orphanage?*"

"Well, you don't have to sound as if it were Outer Mongolia," he drawled in amusement. "It happens, you know. Orphanages do exist."

"I know, but I've never, I mean I don't think I've ever met anyone who was raised in an orphanage."

He grinned. "They've changed a bit since Dickens's time, you know."

"No porridge nowadays?" she hazarded with an attempt at lightness. He obviously didn't want to get serious about that aspect of his past. She wondered just how much orphanages had changed.

"Lumpy oatmeal at times," he admitted, "but plenty of it."

Adena accepted the small joke, sensing it was the end of the discussion. But as she went back to work she thought about what it would be like to be raised in an institution where there couldn't possibly have been enough attention and love to go around. The notion that love was a commodity to be bought like anything else might have been impressed on Holt at a very early age.

"Adena?" She caught the abrupt note of seriousness in the undersea voice.

"Hmmmm?" She hovered over the sauce she was putting together.

"What else did Carrigan accuse you of besides selling me information on the SinTech informant?"

"I'd rather not discuss it, Holt. I told you, he was very upset and said a lot of things he'll probably regret in the morning."

"He accused you of selling yourself to me, didn't he?"

"Are you ready to eat?"

"Adena…" he began aggressively.

"Here, you can carry this tray out to the table. Max, stop begging for more sherry. You look as if your adrenalin has settled down very nicely for the time being."

Holt took the silver serving tray she thrust into his hands, his brows drawing together in an ominous look. But his expression cleared and she knew he'd opted to allow her to change the subject.

"What is it?" he asked, instead, gazing down at the vegetables on the tray.

"Julienne zucchini and carrots in Gorgonzola and walnut sauce," she informed him cheerfully. "We're also having crab soufflés in puff pastry and an endive, beet, and avocado salad. Any complaints?"

"Beats the hell out of lumpy oatmeal. I'll get the wine."

And with that the evening, which had begun so inauspiciously, slipped into a comfortable, homey, and very romantic haze for Adena. By the time she served the coffee and chocolate meringue dessert in the living room, she was even allowing the notion of falling in love with Holt Sinclair to nibble hungrily at the edge of her thoughts.

She sat down on the couch, using a silver server to heap the dessert onto Holt's plate and watched as he finished creating a fire in the modern, white enamel, freestanding fireplace.

He got up, dusting his hands off, and came over to lounge beside her. He picked up his plate with a sigh of contentment.

"Max has never tasted coffee and chocolate meringue, either," Adena noted blandly, glancing at the dog who reposed lazily in front of the fire.

"He's had enough new experiences for one evening," Holt declared.

"You're not going to offer him some of your dessert?"

"My generosity only extends so far," he murmured, forking up a healthy bite.

They finished the dessert in a companionable silence and then, just as Adena was wondering if Holt would try to kiss her, he cradled her against his side with an easy movement that took the tension out of the moment entirely.

"You taste of chocolate," he whispered, tilting her chin upward for a kiss.

"Do you like chocolate?"

"One of my favorite things."

He brushed her mouth again but made no move to initiate a more intimate embrace. Instead, they sat in front of the fire, watching the leaping flames and talking quietly of a variety of inconsequential but pleasant things. Adena pushed aside the thought of how much like a happily married couple they would appear to an outsider.

Then, dangerously, she let the notion slide back into her head. It was a temptation to pretend that Holt was really hers tonight, a temptation to hope that he, too, liked the sense of being "a couple."

And he did nothing to destroy the reckless illusion. When, at long last, he began to seek out the tip of her ear with his lips in a caress that carried the first stirrings of passion, Adena was too far lost in the fantasy to resist.

"Sweetheart," he whispered as he sank his teeth tantalizingly into her earlobe, "when I came through that door tonight I was ready to commit murder. The thought of another man even touching you drives me crazy. I've never felt quite like that before. It made me realize more than ever just how much I want you. Did you mean it last night?"

"Mean what?" she returned unevenly, her head falling back against his arm as it lay behind her on the sofa.

"What you said about wanting me?" he growled, turning his attention to her eyelids. With tiny kisses he closed her lashes for her.

Adena drew in a deep breath, anticipation filling her senses. "Yes." What else could she say at that moment? It was no less than the truth.

"I was so afraid you'd change your mind today, lose your nerve…"

"Having you over for dinner didn't take *that* much courage, Holt," she confessed, barely suppressing her laughter.

He touched the tip of her nose with his tongue. "Didn't it? Not even when you must have guessed what would happen afterward?"

A tingling sensation, which might have been a warning, roused to life somewhere in Adena.

"You won't force yourself on me, Holt," she declared with gentle conviction. But her words didn't banish the tingling radiating through her nerves.

"No," he agreed and said no more.

He stopped her next words with a kiss that began with slow, easy warmth and escalated rapidly into a blaze of urgency.

Quite suddenly Adena realized the comfortable, meandering evening had come to a shattering finish. Holt wanted her, and with this kiss he was telling her just how much.

Her fingers lifted to brace herself, perhaps push him away, but when they touched the softness of the gray cashmere over his shoulders they clung there, searching for the tautly muscled body underneath.

"Holt. Oh, Holt!" she gasped, as he seemed to steal her breath with devastating little kisses.

"Tell me again how much you want me," he commanded huskily. "I want to hear it, I need to hear it. Be generous tonight, sweetheart," he pleaded roughly, and then he was once again invading her mouth.

Adena trembled with rising passion as his tongue invaded her mouth. She couldn't think tonight as he launched his compelling attack on her senses. The whole evening of fantasy had worked against her, leaving her defenseless.

"I want you, Holt." In her mind the confession

was far more honest. I love you, she admitted silently. I have fallen in love with you…!

He groaned against her throat and his hand moved behind her head to the nape of her neck, beginning a seductive massage that made her arch like a kitten.

His other hand covered her fingers as they kneaded his cashmere sweater in a luxurious rhythm. Catching hold of her hand, he guided it under the sweater and inhaled deeply when she responded willingly.

Wrapping her arms around his waist, Adena sought out the feel of his sleek back. She was too caught up in her exploration to protest when he located the buttons on her blouse.

Slowly, with infinite masculine pleasure, Holt undid the tiny pearl fastenings one by one. Adena's anticipation was being stoked higher and higher, so that when he actually touched the nipple of her unconfined breasts she moaned deeply.

As if giving utterance to her passion was a trigger for his own, Holt fell slowly backward on the sofa, pulling her down on top of him. The next thing she knew he had caught the tip of one breast between his lips. She shuddered as he kissed it into a taut peak of feminine desire.

Convulsively, her fingers clenched in his hair as she instinctively held his head close against her.

He slid her blouse aside, stroking the silky skin

of her stomach and cupping the small weight of her soft breasts.

"I need you so much, my sweet Adena. You're so perfect for me."

His tongue wrapped a hardened nipple while his fingers swept around her waist to begin sensuously stroking her spine. Her wine velvet skirt cascaded over his legs as her limbs became entangled with his.

"Ouch!"

"What? What's wrong?" Adena pulled back slightly in concern but Holt was chuckling as he began unbuckling the silver and turquoise belt at her waist.

"Nothing I can't handle," he confided humorously The heavy belt was released and dropped in a glittering pile on the carpet.

"Sorry," she whispered, enjoying the laughter mixed with passion. It was a heady combination, she was discovering.

His eyes met hers and sobered as the silver flames of desire leaped high. "Now that I've started the project," Holt muttered, sliding the opened blouse off her shoulders, "I might as well finish it."

"What project?"

"Undressing you properly."

One by one her garments fell away as if by magic. The only factor which spoiled the illusion was the faint, but definite, trembling of Holt's fingers as he worked. Adena smiled to herself, entranced by this small sign of his own need and vulnerability.

Then he was rolling her lightly aside, getting to his feet, and reaching down to lift her nude body high against his chest.

For a long moment his eyes pored over the figure in his arms, and Adena remembered she was once again wearing a small gold necklace. It was all she had on now. In the pagan firelight did it make him think of her more than ever as a captured slave girl?

Max, with an inborn sense of discretion, politely exited the room.

Six

"You're beautiful by firelight," Holt whispered in a voice that seemed to come from the depths of the sea.

Slowly, carefully, as if she were a jeweled chest he had salvaged from a long lost ship, he settled her on the plush persimmon carpet. Kneeling beside her, his hands moved impatiently on the fastenings of his own clothing but his eyes never left her glowing body.

Adena watched him with an aching wonder, her turquoise gaze partially shielded by passion-heavy lashes. She loved this man, and as he undressed before her she found him attractive beyond reason. She loved him and wanted him.

And there was no denying the power of his own desire for her. It was a potent male magic that swept over them both in shimmering waves, pulling Adena far out to sea.

Golden shadows from the fireplace flickered on the sinewy sleekness of his chest and shoulders as Holt tossed his gray cashmere aside together with his shirt. A moment later he had unclasped his belt and tugged off the remainder of his clothing. The fine trembling in his hand when he reached out to touch her again elicited a feeling of deep tenderness in Adena. At this moment, clothed only in masculine power, Holt was strangely vulnerable.

Without a word Adena opened her arms to the man she loved. He came to her in a rush of need, a nearly soundless groan from deep in his chest an eloquent testimony.

Sprawling heavily along her softness, he seemed to revel in every inch of her just as Adena thrilled to the strength in him. Twining his fingers deep in the thickness of her umber hair, Holt anchored her fiercely still for his kiss.

It was a kiss of total demand and a complex plea. His lips moved on hers, and as her mouth flowered open to receive him, his tongue surged audaciously between her teeth in a symbolic rhythm that set the blood spinning through her veins.

Gold-tinted fingertips danced along Holt's back as

Adena sought the feel of him. When the dance became stronger, a little reckless, and far more urgent, he growled with persuasive encouragement.

"That's it, my sweet Adena. I want you to come apart in my arms tonight. I want to know the full depths of the passion that lies beneath your charm!"

"Holt, please, Holt…" Her throat arched backward and he buried his lips along its delicate, vulnerable line.

"Give yourself to me completely tonight, sweetheart. You'll have no cause to regret it," he swore.

Unconsciously Adena's body lifted against his and he responded by letting her know the strength in his thighs. When her legs writhed tormentedly, he trapped them with his own in an exciting bondage.

She clung to him, moaning deeply, longingly, and when he shifted his weight slightly, she sank her nails convulsively into his muscular male buttock.

"Do you want me now, darling?" he murmured.

"Don't tease me, Holt!"

"Only a little longer, honey," he promised, sliding down the length of her to shower heated kisses over her taut-tipped breasts and across the gentle curve of her stomach.

"Please, Holt!" she begged, clutching at him in a vain effort to force him to complete the union. "Please, darling. I've never felt like this! I'm going out of my mind!"

His tongue licked flames into her navel and then he whispered against the curve of her thigh, "That's what I want you to do. I want you to need me tonight as badly as I need you."

His hand stroked down her leg and moved up along the exquisitely sensitive inside of her thigh, sending a tremor through her.

"Oh!"

Her exclamation was both helpless surrender and a feminine command. Adena's fingers wove little patterns of need over Holt's shoulders, and her hips arched again and again in silent supplication.

At last he made his way back along her body, his touch setting fire to every part of her as he explored and claimed en route. Every curve, every secret place became his. And then he was gently but urgently forcing her legs apart, seeking a place for himself near the heart of her warmth.

"Come to me now, Adena," he rasped, his teeth nipping a little fiercely at the skin of her shoulder. "Open yourself to me and give me what I crave tonight!"

"Yes, yes, my darling Holt," she breathed, drawing him closer as he surged powerfully against her body.

His thick, husky groan of desire mingled with Adena's soft cry of passion. Holt gathered her to him, enveloping her in his heat and aching need. She was swept along on an exultant tide, caught up in a whirlpool that spun her around until the universe threatened to crack.

The only security, the only solidity was Holt, and Adena clung to him as if nothing else in the world mattered.

The irresistible rhythm carried them both to a shattering finish, which wrung a stifled shout of triumph and satisfaction from Holt's throat as Adena shuddered with ecstasy beneath him. The feminine satisfaction in her was every bit as strong as that which had relaxed the body of the man in whose arms she lay.

A long while later Adena stirred languidly against Holt's damp chest, trailing her fingers with idle pleasure through the curling hair.

"You wouldn't be cruel enough to try tickling me when I'm weak and defenseless like this, would you?" he demanded warningly without opening his eyes. She heard the humor in his voice and smiled wickedly.

"Don't tempt me."

"At the moment I'm at your mercy," he groaned. "Just remember, eventually I'll recover."

"To wreak your vengeance upon me for having taken advantage of you?"

"Such a pleasant vengeance," he agreed thoughtfully. Then, quite abruptly, his lazy amusement seemed to evaporate. Propping himself on one elbow, he rose to gaze down into her love-softened face, and his hand splayed possessively across her stomach. Adena discerned a look of possession in his slate-colored eyes, and she wondered if she ought to be more wary of it. Somehow, at this moment, it seemed not threatening but rather a source of security and satisfaction.

"Adena, my lovely Adena," he whispered. She had the feeling that he was searching for the right words and couldn't find them. The force of his emotion was clear, however, and she smiled tremulously up at him.

He lifted his hand from her stomach to touch the circlet of gold at her throat. "You're mine now," he said. "Really and truly mine. My God, sweetheart, I've never wanted a woman the way I wanted you tonight, and I have the feeling that next time it's going to be worse!"

"Worse?" she mocked lightly.

He ignored her attempt at humor. "Next time I'll know for certain what's waiting for me!"

"What is waiting for you?" she asked provocatively.

"I got lost in your arms tonight, sweetheart," he explained, leaning over briefly to kiss the tip of one breast. "And you're a witch to laugh at me for it!"

"I wouldn't think of it!"

"Uh-huh," he muttered skeptically. "Just remember that however much you taunt me, you belong to me. My own sweet slave girl."

"One doesn't own slaves in this day and age, Holt Sinclair," she admonished.

"No?" He sounded disbelieving as he traced the outline of her lips with his forefinger.

"Definitely not! The modern romance is a partnership of equals," she lectured.

"Whatever you say, sweetheart." He kissed the tip of her nose. "I'm a generous man; you're welcome to believe in your own personal fantasies as long as you don't forget the reality behind them."

"*Your* version of reality?" she chuckled.

"Adena, stop playing games with me, sweet witch, and look at me." He waited until she lifted her indulgent turquoise eyes to meet his steady, determined gaze.

"Yes, Holt?" she murmured with suspicious meekness.

"You gave yourself to me tonight," he rasped a little dangerously. "You were meant to belong to me and now you do. From this moment on I have the right to look after you, to take care of you. Do you understand what I'm trying to say?"

"You're asking me to have an affair with you?"

"The affair," he returned thickly, "has already

begun. Adena, I want to hear you say you belong to me…!''

''Talk about catching someone in a weak moment!'' she complained, still unwilling to be totally serious in the luxurious aftermath of his lovemaking.

''I know,'' he admitted, ''but, as I've told you before, I'm a practical man. This somehow seemed like an opportune moment!''

''Businessman that you are, perhaps I should wait until I've read the complete contract,'' she hedged in amusement. ''After all, you once told me I wasn't very clever at bargaining.''

''And tonight hasn't revised my opinion any, either.'' He grimaced wryly.

''What's that supposed to mean?'' she demanded, annoyed.

''I mean you handed everything you had to give over to me without making certain. I intended to be equally generous in return,'' he scolded. But there was a curious satisfaction in his voice.

''You swept me off my feet,'' she complained, laughing up at him.

''You're not going to be serious about this, are you?'' he sighed.

''No.''

''Ah, well, I suppose it doesn't matter,'' he groaned, bending once more to kiss her shoulder.

"Just let me have the words and I'll let you go on cracking jokes all night long."

"The words?" she asked innocently, knowing she would give them to him eventually because they were the truth.

"Let me hear them, Adena," he ordered in a soft growl as he half-smiled down into her eyes.

He really needed them, Adena realized suddenly. He had to hear her make the commitment. How could she deny anything to the man she loved?

"You're a tyrant," she protested, postponing the inevitable a few more seconds.

"I expect most owners of slave girls are."

"I told you the other evening you were going to be difficult to control," she sighed.

"Adena?"

"I'm yours, my darling Holt. If the words are necessary, then take them. I belong to you." Her lips curved invitingly upward. "Just remember, chains like this work both ways!"

He smiled in wicked humor, the satisfaction in him plainly visible. "There's nothing I want more than for you to hold on to me very, very tightly," he agreed and gathered her close again.

He didn't leave until the early hours of the morning, grumbling about having to go home and dress for work. Adena kissed him good-bye at the door,

Max blinking sleepily beside her as he watched his comrade in arms make lingering farewells.

"I'll call you from the office if I can get away to meet you for lunch, all right?" Holt brushed the tip of Adena's brow with a finger.

"Okay," she agreed gently.

"And tomorrow night we'll have dinner at my home. You can bring Max and that way you won't have to come back here afterward," he went on deliberately.

The eyebrow he had been stroking arched faintly as Adena sensed the further commitment which lay behind his suggestion. If he got her into the habit of staying the night it would only be a matter of time before she was moved in completely. They both knew that. Something in her rebelled unhappily at the thought of "playing house" with Holt Sinclair.

"My turn to bring the wine," was all she said.

He kissed her a reluctant good night and then loped lightly down the steps to where the gunmetal gray Ferrari was parked. Adena closed the door and shook her head at Max.

"I hope you know what I'm doing, Max! Because I'm not at all certain that I do!"

But she went back to bed with a sense of well-being she had never known before. Holt Sinclair was a man who could be taught how to love. He just needed a little practice. He was far too accustomed to thinking of life as a series of business transactions. But his lovemaking tonight had left Adena with the feeling that she could change all that. She wasn't sure she had much choice. For her the commitment had been total.

The flowers arrived around eleven o'clock the next morning—a mass of yellow roses, which clashed delightfully with the persimmon carpet and looked instantly at home with the rest of the décor.

Adena inhaled them with delight as she accepted them from the delivery man.

"Oh, thank you!" she breathed as they were thrust into her arms.

"Don't thank me," the young man grinned good-naturedly. "I just deliver. Someone else placed the order!"

She laughed. "I know, but messengers bringing nice things like this deserve their own reward. Speaking of which…" She hurried to rummage through her purse for a suitable tip.

"Thank *you!*" he chuckled, swinging down the steps. Adena knew she had probably overtipped but the knowledge didn't bother her.

The flowers could only be from Holt, she knew, and she set the beauties down on the coffee table and searched for the card.

It was there, along with a simple white box which she hadn't noticed at first. Adena froze as she touched the elegant little package. At once her delight in the flowers dissolved in the embers of a new emotion.

Surely he wouldn't do this to her! Not after last night, she thought shakily. He wouldn't pay her off with an expensive trinket as if she were a mistress who had performed properly and was now to be rewarded!

Her fingers shook as she removed the little white box. Perhaps, she told herself desperately, perhaps it would be a ring…? A ring which was meant to symbolize something meaningful such as an engagement? Yes, yes, she could accept such a gift…

But she knew the box wasn't shaped for a ring. And engagement rings were delivered in person. Her nails bit into her palm as she sat staring at the white box.

All the warm, treasured memories of the previous evening turned cold in her mind as she looked sadly down at the box in her lap. She didn't want to open the deceptive little package. She didn't want to have confirmation of her worst fears.

There was no option, of course. The reality of what last night had meant to Holt had to be faced. He was a man accustomed to paying for love—the only kind of love he knew. He had taken deep pleasure in mastering her emotions. Which meant, she thought hysterically, she had probably been well paid!

With a wrench, she lifted the top of the box, and with trembling fingers she unfolded the elegant inner wrapping.

It was a gold collar for her neck. A sophisticated, incredibly beautiful thing of delicate lines, and it was finished with three glittering diamonds that would fit into the hollow at the base of her throat.

Adena could have wept. With nerveless fingers she opened the silver card inscribed with her name in a careless, bold hand.

For the one who now belongs to me, she read. It was signed with a slashing *H*. Slowly she crumpled the card in her hand, turning to look at Max's questioning face with an expression of pain.

"How could he do this to me, Max? After all I thought we shared last night, how could he treat me as if I were an expensive prostitute? A woman whose love he can buy?"

Max pushed his face sympathetically into her lap, his dark eyes worried. It had been easy to help his lady last night; a dog could deal with overt rudeness. But there was nothing he could do this morning. He did not even understand.

As the pain coalesced in her, it turned into something else. Adena rose to her feet as the searing hurt became an equally searing anger. She held the box in her hand, staring at it as if it were a time bomb. Then she stuffed the crumpled card inside and slammed the lid shut.

"How dare he?" she whispered tightly to the anxious dog. "How *dare* he? If he thinks I'll let him get away with this!"

She bit off her own words as she picked up the phonebook and searched for a messenger service. Then she was dialing the phone with trembling fingers, her anger at such a pitch that she had to exercise extreme control over her voice when she spoke to the dispatching agent on the other end.

In a few minutes everything was arranged. She hung up the phone and picked up a piece of paper on which she tried to write a message to be returned to Holt along with his "gift."

It took three tries before she was able to get the simple words down on paper. She wrapped the package, inserted the note, and waited for the messenger to arrive at her front door.

Twenty minutes later the box was gone, carrying her note with it. *I thought you could afford me,* she had written in seething anger, *but this proves you can't.*

As she watched the messenger drive off, Adena ignored the tearing sensation in her heart. Slowly she turned from the window and faced Max.

"I think," she began very carefully, "that it's

time you and I had that vacation I promised a couple of days ago, Max. Don't worry, you're going to love the country life!''

Two hours later she was nearly packed. The polished-looking tweeds and flannels that Adena imagined looked right for walking Max in the country were hanging in a clothes bag that was thrown over a small, red leather suitcase by the door. Max, sensing they were on the move, waited patiently beside the suitcase as Adena ran through a list of country inns she'd found advertised in a magazine which focused on California life-styles.

It was annoying to find many of them already booked. Deliberately, she crossed off one entry after another until at last she found one which had just been informed of a cancellation.

"Yes, you can bring the dog," a cheery voice on the other end assured her, "and don't forget, the price of the room includes breakfast!"

Adena thanked the woman and hung up the phone with a sigh of relief. She had begun to think escape was going to prove a little more difficult than it should be under the circumstances.

"It's all settled, Max. Let's be on our way. I'll just tell Mrs. Harrison next door that we're going to be gone for a few days and then we'll..."

She broke off with a start as the doorbell chimed and Max pricked up his ears interestedly. Adena sat staring at the door, intuition warning her who was on the other side. If it hadn't, Max's welcoming bark would have.

Before she lost her courage, she leaped to her feet, flew across the room, and flung open the door with a resounding crash.

"You've got a hell of a lot of nerve, Holt Sinclair, showing up on my doorstep!" she blazed fiercely up at him.

He stood gazing down at her taut features, holding the damning white box in one hand. In his dark, conservatively tailored business suit, and with his sable hair gleaming from the small rain shower through which he had walked, he seemed very dangerous and menacing as he filled her doorway. His gray eyes were as hard as slate.

He raked her figure, taking in her gray flannel slacks, black sweater, and suede jacket. Then his gaze flickered to the suitcase and clothes bag at his feet.

"Going somewhere, Adena?" he asked in a dark voice that told her he was as coldly angry as she was blazingly furious.

"As a matter of fact, I am!" She would not let him intimidate her. "Max and I are going to the country. We want to get away for a while!"

He stepped into the room, crowding her aside and

closing the door behind him. "You seem to be forgetting something," he grated.

"If you mean that…that *trinket* you sent over this morning, don't worry about it! It doesn't go with anything I own!"

"Really?" he drawled. "I thought it would go beautifully with something *I* own! But never mind. If it's not sufficient, there's more where it came from!"

"More! *More!*" Adena's voice rose on a frustrated shriek. "How dare you insult me like this!"

"There aren't many women in the world who would consider this little item an insult! But if there aren't enough diamonds in it for you, I can always take it back and choose something else!"

Adena couldn't find the words. So she slapped him instead with all her might. It was a full, open-handed blow which he took with mocking indifference, even though it left the reddening imprint of her fingers on his tanned cheek and brought another shade of red to his cheekbones.

"There's no need to take it back," she raged as he made no move to counter the slap. "I'm sure one of your other women will be more than happy to accept it. But my price for last night's services is a hell of a lot higher, Holt Sinclair."

"Name it," he snarled.

Adena flinched a little beneath the impact of his

words. She had a feeling he was barely restraining himself from throttling her.

"Why should I bother? You can't afford it!"

At that, he did take hold of her, one hand reaching out to grasp her shoulder and haul her up against his chest. "I said, *name it!*"

"You fool!" For the first time some of the anger in her reverted to pain as his fingers dug into her shoulder. Tears dampened her turquoise eyes as she stared up at him. His rage began to beat at her, destroying her anger, leaving only sadness and humiliation. "You idiot! You didn't have to waste your money on gold and diamonds. Can't you understand? What I gave you last night, I gave for free. Gratis! No charge! For nothing! But you insisted on repaying me with an insult of the first magnitude, didn't you?"

"*Insult!* Adena, what are you talking about?"

"I'm talking about that damned necklace! The necklace you're holding in your hand. The one that arrived this morning and made me feel like a prostitute! A kept woman!"

"Are you out of your mind?" he raged, some of the slate-coldness in his eyes changing to uncertainty. "Adena, this was a gift..."

"Of course it was! Bought at the same expensive place you buy all your mistresses' gifts, I imagine! But I'm not accepting your payment for services rendered, Holt. Can't you understand? There are some things you can't buy in this world, and I'm one of them!"

"Oh, my God," he breathed in disgust. "I don't believe this! Adena, stop yelling at me and listen."

"I don't want to listen to you. I don't *have* to listen to you! Regardless of what you think, you don't own me, Holt Sinclair. I don't care how many gold and diamond necklaces you buy me!"

He pressed her face into his suit jacket, muffling her words. Wrapping his arms around her tightly, he kept her pinned helplessly against his chest.

"Adena, this wasn't meant as a payment for last night, damn it! I bought the necklace because I wanted to give you something. It was a gift for you, nothing more or less. Surely a man is allowed to buy his woman presents? The necklace was supposed to arrive with yellow roses..." He glanced around the room and spotted them sitting on the coffee table. "I see you didn't throw them away. Why not? Is it somehow all right to accept roses but not necklaces?"

"Yes!" she shouted into his jacket.

She felt the tension go out of him and knew his mouth was curving upward in a small smile.

"Then next time I'll have to order the necklace's equivalent in roses, won't I?" he murmured into her hair. "It's going to be a lot of flowers!"

"Don't be ridiculous!" she seethed.

"You're the one who's being ridiculous. I was on top of the world this morning. I felt like a conquering hero; the victorious general at the gates of the city; master of all I surveyed. Is it any wonder I wanted to give something to the woman who made me feel that way?"

"You're so accustomed to paying for things!" she wailed, wilting a little against his hard frame.

"It was a gift, Adena. Can't you understand that?" he soothed, his hand stroking her hair.

"With you there's too fine a line between a gift and a payment!"

"Give me a chance, honey," he begged persuasively. "You're overreacting to the whole situation. You misinterpreted everything!"

"I'm not so sure about that," she muttered.

"Darling, I'm going to enjoy giving you nice things from time to time and I can afford to. Don't treat my gifts as payoffs!"

The remainder of the fire went out of Adena, and she was horrified to find herself snuffling against his jacket. She tried to pull away and he let her put a couple of inches between them. Looking up at him through her lashes, Adena studied him with tear-dampened eyes.

He smiled ruefully down into her uncertain face. "And please don't send any more of my gifts back the way you did this necklace. You gave me a shock from which I'm still recovering." His gray eyes darkened for an instant as he remembered his fury. "All I can say is, it's a damn good thing I had to drive a ways to get my hands on you. It gave me some time to calm down."

"No more necklaces, Holt," Adena began with a deep breath. "I mean it. I don't want gold and diamonds and expensive gifts from you. I don't want beautiful gifts like that one."

He stared at her, the expression on his face turning from wry relief to an enigmatic look. "Adena, be reasonable. It's natural for a man to give things to the woman he…"

Holt faltered briefly over the next word and sudden hope soared in Adena's heart. But it crashed an instant later.

"The woman he wants, the woman who belongs to him. You can't refuse me that privilege."

"Yes, I can," she replied stonily.

"Adena…!"

"I don't trust you, Holt."

"You don't trust me!" She sensed renewed anger in him.

"I don't trust you to know the difference between making payments and giving gifts. So no more presents like that necklace."

"Damn it, Adena, this is ridiculous! I won't let you..."

The ringing of the telephone cut off his next words, and he reluctantly released her so she could answer it.

Feeling his intent, determined gaze on her all the way, Adena moved toward the telephone and lifted the receiver. She spoke quietly into it for a few moments and then replaced it.

"It looks like my plans for getting away to the country are going to have to wait," she said slowly as she turned to meet Holt's gaze. "That was a call in response to my résumé. I've been asked to come for an interview this afternoon."

"What company?" Holt demanded shortly.

She told him and he nodded. "It's a good firm. You'd better go ahead with the interview."

"Yes," she agreed, wondering why he appeared so instantly satisfied with the turn of events. Probably because it meant she couldn't leave town, Adena decided grimly.

Some of the tension in the room disappeared, only to be replaced by the unpleasant nervousness that goes with job interviews. Just what she needed after such an unsettling morning, Adena thought ruefully.

"I'll take Max out for a walk while you get ready," Holt offered.

Max, obviously relieved to have things simmering

down to normal, reacted quickly to the sound of his name.

"You have to go back to work," Adena protested.

"I'll go after I've walked Max. Calm down, honey," he added with a reassuring smile. "You'll knock 'em dead! Come on, Max, where's your leash?"

"Er, Holt?"

"Hmmm?" He had found the leather leash hanging by the door and was leaning down to snap it onto Max's collar.

"There are certain things about walking a dog in the city..."

"What's this?" He looked blankly down at the plastic gadget and bag she was holding out to him.

"Guess," she suggested dryly.

"You mean I'm supposed to...?"

"Have fun."

Seven

$\textbf{M}$ax and Holt hadn't returned by the time Adena changed into a small, tailored loden green business suit and a pair of bronze-toned pumps. She stood in front of the bedroom mirror, running a brush briskly through her hair and frowned intently into the glass. Where were they? The thought of Holt dutifully picking up after Max was the only bright spot in what had turned out to be a disaster of a day!

Well, she couldn't wait for them. She would leave a note on the door, telling Holt to get the key from Mrs. Harrison. Adena picked up the shoulder bag which matched her pumps and headed for the door.

A few minutes later she was catching the bus for

the bustling financial district north of Market Street. Holt was right, Adena thought ruefully as she glanced down at the address in her lap. The company which had called so unexpectedly was a good one. It would be a stroke of the greatest luck to land a job with such a firm so easily!

She got off the bus near the Pacific Coast Stock Exchange on Pine Street and walked the short distance to the prestigious building which housed the company's headquarters. Deliberately she tried to calm her frazzled mind and pull together a proper attitude for a job interview. Unfortunately, she kept thinking about Holt.

But once inside the towering monolith of a building, the pressure of the business at hand took over. She was ushered politely into a plush personnel office and the interview began.

Within a very short time it became apparent that the position being filled would suit her very well. Adena's enthusiasm grew, and so did that of the interviewer. She was a perfect match for the job description in terms of experience and qualifications.

The wonderful sense of good fortune gave Adena an extra burst of enthusiasm, which successfully hid the remainder of her morning's unhappiness.

These people really seemed to want her, she thought with a rush of pleasant surprise.

"I'm going to take you up to meet with Mr. Olson, Miss West," the professionally cordial man from the personnel department said as he rose to his feet. "Olson is in charge of our accounting department, and he is the man to whom you will be reporting if you are hired by us."

Adena smiled her thanks and followed the interviewer up to the fourteenth floor, to the attractive, subdued offices of the accounting department.

"Ah, yes, Miss West! I'm so pleased to meet you. Your résumé hit my desk this morning, and things certainly look like an excellent fit on paper." Harvey Olson, a dapper, middle-aged man with thinning gray hair and a cheerful smile greeted her as if she were a long-lost associate.

"Take your time with Miss West and send her back to me when you've finished," the personnel officer instructed with a farewell nod as he closed the door.

"Well, well, Miss West," Olson began jovially, resuming his seat and beaming across the wide mahogany desk at her. "I'm sure you must be brimming with questions. Why don't we start with a few of them?"

"I'd appreciate that, Mr. Olson," Adena began, composing herself to ask all the important things while still managing to sound like an intelligent, enthusiastic, and otherwise ideal candidate. Interview-

ing was such a strain, she reflected. Her whole day
had been a strain!

But she really couldn't complain about this particular interview, she decided practically. It was rapidly becoming obvious that a plum of a job was
about to fall right into her lap.

It wasn't until very nearly the end of the meeting
with Harvey Olson that Adena inadvertently made a
remark that left her not with a plum in her lap, but
a small grenade.

"I think you're going to fit in here awfully well,
Miss West," Olson was saying with a pleased nod.

"The position sounds very exciting," Adena
agreed honestly enough. "Your firm seems to have
an excellent advancement program and I like the
variety to which I'll be exposed. Internal auditing
intrigues me, and I'll look forward to gaining more
experience with it."

"Excellent, excellent. I think that about wraps it
up. I'll give a call down to Thornton, the man who
brought you up here." Olson winked conspiratori-
ally. "Personnel reserves the right to make the official offers, you know. I wouldn't want to step on
any toes by jumping the gun, but just between you
and me..."

"Well, I'm sure they'll want to complete a few
of the basic formalities," Adena chuckled politely,
"such as officially checking for references..." She

could only be grateful that Carrigan Labs handled all reference checks through their own Personnel Department and didn't refer requests to individuals in the company. If she were lucky, Jeff Carrigan would never know she'd found a new job!

"Oh, I think we can skip the reference checks," Harvey Olson declared regally. "After all, we've already received a recommendation from a respected source!"

"I beg your pardon?" Adena looked at him blankly.

Olson laughed easily. "Come now, no need to be embarrassed about having someone like Holt Sinclair providing a personal recommendation. He wouldn't have done it unless he thought you were right for us, and my boss has a tremendous amount of respect for Sinclair's judgment."

"Holt Sinclair?" Adena breathed, chilled. "He asked you to hire me?"

"No, no, of course not!" Olson chuckled dismissingly. "He simply found out we were looking for someone and called one of our vice-presidents— who happens to be my boss—and said he knew someone who would probably be perfect. Personnel checked, and since your résumé had just arrived, it got hustled along to my office."

"I see. I hadn't realized..." Adena found herself remembering the way she had blithely told Holt where she had sent her résumés; then she recalled his look of satisfaction that morning after she'd hung up the phone and told him who had called.

"We're always grateful to get the opinion of someone like Sinclair," Harvey Olson went on conversationally as he picked up the phone and dialed the office of Adena's initial interviewer.

Bleakly she sat there and listened to Olson's side of the conversation, trying to recover from her shock.

The first thing that crystallized in her mind was that Holt had made another move to buy her. He was arranging the "gift" of a job.

How *dare* he? she thought as the morning's anger rekindled. What would it take to teach a lesson to a man who was prepared to pay for anything and everything he wanted? How could she ever get it through his one-track mind that Adena West wasn't a commodity he could purchase with gold necklaces and job security?

Damn the man! How would he feel if she were to pay him off for his attention and prowess in bed?

Yes! she thought furiously, how would he feel if she could somehow turn the tables. She knew exactly how he'd react, she told herself grimly. He'd be furious. His pride would be lacerated and he'd be livid with fury. In short, he'd know exactly how she was feeling today!

With only half-hearted attention that no one seemed to notice, Adena went politely through the rest of the interview formalities. When the expected offer was made, she promised to think it over and let the company know in a week's time. By the time she walked back out onto the busy sidewalks of the financial district, her mind was made up. Holt Sinclair was overdue for a serious lesson in interpersonal relationships!

She was on her way to the smart, expensive shops near Union Square before she'd given herself time to change her mind. It would cost a fortune to do it right, but that really wasn't too serious a consideration. There was absolutely no doubt in Adena's mind that Holt would be far too incensed to ever accept the "gift."

The thought of him demanding that she take it back brought a grim satisfaction. Perhaps when he found himself in the same boat she'd been in this morning, he would think twice about insulting her with one payoff after another!

To make a suitable impact, it was going to have to be a truly elegant present, she decided as she turned briskly into an expensive jewelry store. A gift of definite, undeniable value. One he couldn't possibly accept and one that would infuriate him.

As soon as she saw the watch lying on velvet under the polished glass countertop, Adena knew she'd found the ideal weapon for her revenge. No, not revenge, she reminded herself as she asked to see the watch; she wasn't lowering herself to the level of plotting revenge. She was teaching Holt Sinclair a valuable lesson! The thought of his certain anger at being taught that lesson was simply a satisfying side effect.

It was a handsome timepiece. Adena stared at it for a long moment. Handcrafted in Switzerland of eighteen-karat gold, it shone with a subdued richness and sophistication that spoke volumes. It had an electronic quartz movement housed in a case so elegantly thin that it defied the imagination. It was perfect.

As she wrote out the check that would drain her savings account horribly, were it ever cashed, Adena had a fleeting thought of how nice it would be to really give such a beautiful watch to Holt. She pushed the thought aside at once. She certainly couldn't afford such generosity on a continuing basis!

She swallowed a little as she handed over the check and told the salesman where to send the watch. Holt would be receiving it in his office before the afternoon was over.

Which meant, Adena quickly calculated, that he would be sending the watch back first thing in the morning. And that, in turn, meant the huge check

could be stopped before it was actually cashed. Tomorrow morning was Saturday, so Monday morning
everything could be cancelled safely.

It was only as she rode the bus home that Adena's
temper finally succumbed to a few tremors of unpleasant anticipation. Holt was going to be *very* upset. The thought of him yelling at her as she pointed
out that he was feeling exactly as she had that morning was not a pleasant prospect. Still, it would all
be worth it.

The real question, of course, was whether he really would learn the lesson she intended. Could he
finally be made to understand how disturbing it was,
how *humiliating* it was to be bought? To have one's
favors paid for as if one were a mistress or, in his
case, a kept man?

Still simmering with righteous satisfaction, Adena
let herself into her apartment, remembering the note
she had enclosed with the watch. *For Holt,* she had
written bravely, *with thanks for the job hunting as-
sistance and various and assorted events by firelight.*

It had been a cheeky, saucy, deliberately insulting
little note. She didn't want him to misunderstand.
The fabulously expensive watch would say the rest.
Perhaps she should have enclosed it with flowers...?

Dwelling on the various possibilities inherent in
the situation she had just created, Adena took a mo-

ment or two to realize that Max was not at the door greeting her.

Good grief! Max and Holt couldn't still be out walking? No, they had come and gone, she realized as she picked up a piece of paper lying on the coffee table near the yellow roses. She recognized Holt's sprawling hand at once. Talk about saucy notes! She read his message.

Max is fine. I took him back to Sausalito with me, where he will be eagerly awaiting your arrival later this evening. You did remember you both were invited to dinner, didn't you, darling? We're also going to have to put in an appearance at a business cocktail party afterward, so wear something appropriate. I'll pick you up when I leave the office this afternoon. Around five.

P.S. In case you haven't guessed, I'm holding Max as assurance for your good behavior.

P.P.S. I think he's in love with the lady poodle two blocks from your flat. Remind me to tell you about it this evening.

Yours,
Holt

Adena crumpled the note with a stifled groan. In that

moment of frustration and anger there was a terrible impulse to laugh. He'd kidnapped Max!

He probably thought it all very humorous, but she wondered how long he'd be amused after the watch arrived. And that event shouldn't take long, she reflected grimly, glancing at the clock. SinTech's offices were in downtown San Francisco, not far from Carrigan Labs, in fact.

She spent the rest of the day in a state of wariness, jumping whenever the phone rang. But Holt never called. She was beginning to wonder if perhaps the watch hadn't been delivered when she finally gave up pacing the floor and started to dress for dinner. She could only go on the assumption now that he would, indeed, show up after work. She'd have to act as if everything were all right, as if giving a man a frightfully expensive gold watch to thank him for his favors constituted normal behavior.

With an almost defiant air, Adena chose an opulent gold-shot silk paisley dress done in deep jewel tones that complemented her eyes, which were shining with an unnatural brightness. She chose burnished gold evening shoes and ignored the necklace Holt had given her when she selected her jewelry. The incriminating little white box had been left pointedly near the flowers. Adena didn't touch it.

Shortly after five, clothed in all the sophistication she could muster under the circumstances, Adena went back to pacing the persimmon carpet. Was he going to show or not? Had he received the watch or not? Was he in a fury over it or not? *Why* hadn't he called or driven back to her flat in a rage?

Adena thought her nerves were going to snap under the increasing pressure, and when the doorbell finally rang she had a sudden impulse to run in the opposite direction.

Perhaps the watch hadn't arrived, she told herself. Perhaps this evening would go off with a reasonable degree of normality.

The instant she opened the door with trembling fingers, her chin lifted in unconscious defiance, Adena knew Holt had gotten the watch.

He was wearing it!

His strong, tanned hand was braced casually against the door frame as she jerked open the door. His crisp white cuff had fallen back far enough to reveal the thin, elegant gold watch on his sinewy wrist.

Adena stared at that wrist in fascination for a second, unable to believe her eyes.

"It's beautiful," Holt drawled deeply. "It's the most beautiful gift anyone has ever given me. Come to think of it, it's about the only gift anyone has ever given me. I always seem to be the one on the giving rather than the getting end."

Slowly, as if hypnotized, Adena dragged her

stunned gaze away from the subtly gleaming watch, along the length of the sleeve of Holt's suit, and up to the gray mists of his eyes. She swallowed dryly.

"You like it?"

"I have only one objection," he murmured, lowering his hand and stepping through the door.

"Yes?" She couldn't believe this!

"You should have had it inscribed." He cupped her pale face between gently rough hands and kissed her soundly. "I'd like something suitably mushy on the back of the case, I think. Will that be all right?"

"Holt…"

"Thank you, Adena," he murmured, smiling down into her wide eyes. "I shall treasure it always."

"Holt…" Adena couldn't find the right words, so she tried again. "Holt, I bought that…"

"I know you did, darling. I got the card. I suppose I should say you shouldn't have, but how can I do that when I had so much pleasure from selecting that necklace this morning? No woman would give a watch like this to a man unless she really cared for him. It must have cost you a fortune!"

"As a matter of fact…" she began, seeing an opening.

"But now that you've landed yourself a new position, I guess you can afford it. And I'm too entranced with my gift to tell you that you shouldn't have spent so much money on me.''

Adena felt as if she were sinking into quicksand. He was taking her expensive "lesson" all wrong! He thought she'd wanted to give him the watch because she cared for him.

"I'm glad you finally realized that my gift to you was not an insult," he went on cheerfully with a warmth in his gray eyes that defeated her. "I must say, this was a hell of an apology, though! I certainly never expected anything on this order."

"Yes, well, I..."

"We can talk more about it at dinner. I'm afraid it's not going to be Annie's home cooking tonight, though, except for Max. When I remembered that business party tonight I decided we'd have an early dinner down at Ghirardelli Square. Let's go, honey. I want to hear all about your interview this afternoon. I take it from the note with the watch that it went pretty well, hmmm?"

Helplessly swept along on the tide of Holt's interpretation of her "gift," Adena allowed herself to be helped into the Ferrari and driven to the old chocolate factory complex which had been restored to contain an enticing miscellany of shops, art galleries, theaters and restaurants. Panic raised its ugly head as Holt settled her gallantly across from him at an intimate table for two and began guiding the conversation. She was going to have to say something to set the record straight—but what?

"Holt," she began firmly as the first course arrived, "you shouldn't have encouraged your friend to have Mr. Olson interview me...."

"Nonsense. When you told me you'd sent in a résumé, I called up to see what kind of openings they had. I talked to Cal Masters a bit and told him I thought I knew the ideal candidate. He took it from there."

"But, Holt, don't you see, you shouldn't have...."

"Honey, you'd already sent in your résumé, hadn't you?" he pointed out with great logic. "All I did was hurry things along a little. That's enough about that. I knew you'd get the job. Tell me when you decided to buy me this watch?"

She blinked uncertainly at the little-boy enthusiasm in him and wondered how to explain. It was becoming increasingly clear to her that giving a gift to a man who probably had grown up without receiving very many at all was definitely not the right approach to teaching him the lesson she'd wanted him to learn. He was too excited by the novelty of a present to see just what it meant.

"The idea," she declared bluntly, "came to me shortly after I found out you'd had a hand in getting me that job interview!"

He nodded equably. "Nice of you to feel grateful for that, but to tell you the truth, I liked the part in the note where you implied that what we had last night in front of your fireplace meant something really special to you." He leaned forward with a warm, intimate expression that made her catch her breath. "Because it meant a great deal to me, too. When you went out and bought this watch you must have been feeling exactly the way I did when I picked out that necklace this morning."

Oh my God! Adena thought. What was she going to do? She felt as if she were being sucked further and further down into the depths of the sea. How did one say it was all a mistake, that the watch had to be returned or she would be nearly broke? Visions of having to sell off a large portion of her slowly developing stock portfolio raced through her brain.

With suppressed hysteria, Adena saw herself having to accept the position for which she'd interviewed today in order to stay financially afloat, and it was all because she couldn't find the courage to tell Holt the watch had to be returned before the jeweler cashed her check!

It was ridiculous, but as the evening progressed it became more and more difficult to summon the nerve to explain the whole disaster. Holt loved his watch. He thoroughly enjoyed the idea of Adena having selected it for him, and he was busy composing little messages to have engraved on the back of the gold case. His gray eyes slid to the gleam of gold every time there was an occasion to extend his arm, and he consulted the new timepiece more frequently than necessary throughout the evening.

Adena was trapped, and shortly before the dessert arrived she silently admitted it to herself. Her scheme had backfired. She was going to have to face that and not give in to panic. True, the watch was expensive, but it wasn't really going to wipe out her savings account. Checking account, yes, but not her savings. Monday morning she would transfer some cash from her money-market fund to her checking account. That would cover the rent and other necessities for the coming month. Mentally she did calculations and decided she wasn't going to starve to death.

Talk about teaching someone a lesson, she thought grimly. She'd certainly learned one herself tonight. Never give something you couldn't afford!

She tried to tell herself it was only pride that stood between her and renewed financial solvency, but she knew better. She knew her inability to tell Holt the truth rested on the fact that she didn't have the heart to wipe the deep, satisfied pleasure from his eyes. She loved him. The watch had made him happy and she couldn't bear to tell him it had been intended for another purpose altogether.

The acceptance of her fate prodded Adena into accepting another glass of the gorgeous Amador County Zinfandel wine Holt had ordered earlier. It was symbolic, she decided, that the wine came from the slopes of the California gold country where she had been planning to escape to her quaint little inn.

"Oh, no!"

"What's wrong, honey?" Holt studied her look of consternation.

"I didn't cancel my reservation at the inn! I got so involved with the job interview and the...the watch that I forgot to phone the manager and tell her I couldn't make it after all!"

"Oh, that. Don't worry about it. I saw the number by the phone and called her for you before I spirited Max off to Sausalito."

She looked at him resentfully. "Thank you," Adena told him a little acidly. "Speaking of my stolen dog..."

"That's right, I was going to tell you about the affair he's trying to get started with that poodle, wasn't I? Poor Max, I know just what he's going through. That poodle is going to be nothing but trouble at first."

"Perhaps he'll arrange to have a particularly juicy bone delivered to her front door," Adena suggested, taking another sip of wine. The thinly veiled sarcasm was lost on Holt.

"I'll suggest it to him. Ready to go? I want to get the party over with so we can go home and relax."

Adena was still trying to figure out how she was going to tell Holt she had no intention of spending the night with him in Sausalito when they walked into the polished, expensively catered party being given in one of Nob Hill's luxurious hotels.

The whole day, she reflected fatalistically, was turning out to be a case of one thing after another. When the tray of champagne came by, she helped herself. She deserved it.

"Darling, I'd like you to meet John Rawlins," Holt was saying smoothly as a distinguished older man made his way toward them through the crowd of well-dressed people. "John is a client of Sin-Tech's."

Adena smiled, automatically acknowledging the introduction. As soon as it was over, there were more to come. She was on her third glass of champagne, and thinking of how well she was functioning under the circumstances, when Holt's conversation with another business acquaintance who designed computers was interrupted by a ravishing blonde dressed in skintight silver lamé.

"Holt, darling! How good to see you. I was hoping you would be able to make it tonight... And who's your quiet little friend?" The brilliantly made-up blue eyes which turned to gaze at Adena weren't unkind, but the "quiet little friend" had been pushed rather far in the course of the day.

"This is Adena West," Holt was saying with the cool male pride of possession. His gray eyes gleamed down at her as he made the introduction. "Adena, this is Charlotte Michaels, a business associate of mine."

Adena returned Charlotte's smile with a determinedly polite one and resisted the impulse to say "I'll bet."

"How do you do, Charlotte. What sort of business are you in?"

"I'm a sales rep for some of the raw materials Holt's firm uses," the friendly, charming, very beautiful Charlotte informed her readily.

Adena was thinking of Charlotte and raw materials when the blonde suddenly exclaimed over the rich gold on Holt's wrist as he handed her a glass off a passing tray.

"How fabulous, Holt! I've been looking at watches like that myself. A new acquisition, isn't it? That company makes a lovely feminine model that I'd give my right arm to own!"

"Marvelous technology, isn't it?" remarked the man with whom Holt had been talking before the advent of Charlotte. "Incredible what the Swiss have done with quartz movements." He, too, looked at the watch on Holt's wrist.

"Adena gave it to me," Holt announced proudly, slicking back his cuff to provide a better view. "Beautiful, isn't it?"

"Adena gave it to you?" Charlotte murmured with a sudden glance of pure feminine speculation in her vivid blue eyes.

"What did you ever do to deserve that?" John Rawlins asked, wandering over from where he had been standing with a group of executives. He, too, joined the small group of admirers who were glancing from the watch to Adena.

Afterward she would blame it on having had too much champagne on top of the Zinfandel wine. She would also seek to explain what happened next as the inevitable result of a day which had been a disaster from start to finish. In fact, Adena would later think of a thousand and one excuses, none of which would suffice for her next words.

She took one look at the group of friendly, curious, questioning faces wanting to know what the occasion had been for the giving of the handsome gold watch and she said quite clearly, "It was an engagement present."

Eight

The silence in the Ferrari was awesome.

As the gunmetal gray car sped through the night, Adena sat very still and thought about such unnerving things as twists of fate, destiny, and the fools people made of themselves. The lights of the city, glowing behind a thin blanket of curling fog, lent an otherworldly atmosphere to the scene outside the car window, an atmosphere which seemed to emphasize Adena's sensation of being trapped.

She was going to have to say something, she knew. It was obviously up to her to break the terrible silence. Holt's profile, harshly etched in the lights of the instrument panel, indicated he had no intention of being the first to speak. And someone had to say something!

Adena got a grip on her jittery nerves. "Holt?" She winced inwardly as she heard the uncertain, tremulous note in her voice.

"Hmmm?"

He sounded as if he were paying her only polite, somewhat absent, attention, she thought disgustedly.

"Holt, I'm sorry. I don't know what got into me. I went crazy! I...I've had a very upsetting day and I think I had a little too much to drink tonight, and everything just sort of went out of control there for a minute." She broke off, listening, appalled, to her own words. "I guess. I mean, I don't know what made me say it..."

"You don't?" His attention was still on the late evening traffic and he gave her the impression they were involved in some mildly desultory conversation. Adena began to get angry. It was a welcome counter to the embarrassment and chagrin in which she had been wallowing.

"Holt, I'm trying to apologize," she bit out, staring straight ahead. "And it's not as if it were all my fault!"

"Wasn't it?"

"We could have gotten out of the whole mess very nicely if you'd just laughed it off! Made a joke out of it!" she accused wretchedly. "You didn't have to stand there and agree with me, for heaven's sake!''

"It seemed the most logical thing to do at the time.''

"Oh, my God!'' Adena collapsed into the corner of the seat in disgust, her mind all too vividly alive with memories of what had happened after Holt had done the "most logical thing.'' The round of congratulations and enthusiastic questions, which had continued until Holt had mercifully excused both of them, would haunt her mind for years, she was sure of it.

The hard line of Holt's mouth crooked faintly upward although he didn't turn his head to look at her. "Are you trying to tell me you didn't mean anything serious when you gave me this watch, Adena?'' he asked quite gently.

"Serious! Of course I meant something serious,'' she snapped, goaded enough to bring the whole thing out in the open and correct his misunderstanding of her gift.

"Just as I meant something serious with that necklace,'' he murmured before she could launch into a tirade on the real reason she'd nearly bankrupted herself to buy a watch.

His words threw her for an instant. Adena blinked suspiciously as she eyed his profile.

"Don't try telling me you gave me that necklace

as an engagement present," she hissed. "You know damn well you had no such notion in mind at the time!"

"No," he agreed a little too readily for Adena's liking. "But at the time I didn't know how much you cared…"

"How much *I* cared!"

"It's all right, honey," he soothed, "you don't have to be afraid to admit it. Besides, you already *have* admitted it." He glanced meaningfully at the gleaming gold watch on his left wrist. "Now that I know how you feel about me, why shouldn't we get married?"

"Why shouldn't we get married! Holt, you don't just go into something like that without a great deal of…of thought and love and…"

"If we don't get married we're going to wind up living together. You know that as well as I do. You want me and I want you."

"You're rushing to all the wrong conclusions," Adena began a little wildly.

He sent her a sidelong glance. "Are you telling me you didn't mean anything with the watch?"

The feeling of being trapped grew stronger. Adena saw the future diving down a long tunnel from which there was no escape. She knew beyond a shadow of a doubt that she couldn't bring herself to explain the real reason she'd given Holt the watch.

She loved him, and his deep pleasure in the gift was something she couldn't reach out and crush. How many gifts had he received in his life, she wondered. An orphan who went on to become a self-made man in a rough world where everything had its price. No, such a man probably hadn't received many presents.

"Of course I meant something when I gave you the watch," she muttered defensively. "I...I'm glad you like it."

"I shall treasure it always," he murmured.

"But it wasn't meant to have any strings attached," she went on bravely. "I wasn't trying to push you into marriage."

"I know that. But now that the idea has come up I don't see any reason why we shouldn't go ahead with it." His voice darkened with a sensual shading. "I want you, Adena. One way or another I'm going to have you with me. I think, all things considered, marriage is the logical answer."

"But, Holt...!"

"Don't worry, sweetheart, I'll take care of everything."

Feeling confused, shaken, and much too fuzzy-headed because of the wine, Adena tried to come up with a logic equal to his own. But it was terribly difficult, because deep down she loved him too much to pretend to herself that she didn't want marriage.

But marriage to a man who didn't understand about love? Who thought lovers could be bought? A man who frankly admitted he only wanted her? Face it, Adena told herself resolutely, he certainly hadn't mentioned marriage before she had made that horrible faux pas this evening!

Then, with blinding clarity, Adena realized what was happening. Holt was tacitly agreeing to pay her price—the price he assumed she was asking in exchange for giving herself to him!

It was the only explanation that made sense to her muddled brain at that moment. He wanted her and he was willing to pay for the things he wanted in life. She had rejected his necklace this morning and then, not very subtly, let him know that what she really was after was a wedding ring. He thought he now understood her price.

Bemused and shocked by the end result of her reasoning, Adena didn't become fully aware of her surroundings until she realized the Ferrari was on the approach to the Golden Gate Bridge.

"Where are we going?" she demanded forcefully, sitting up straight.

"Home. It's getting late and you know how Max disapproves of late hours." Holt smiled.

"Holt, take me back to my apartment," Adena ordered grimly. "I'm not spending the night with you."

"Why not?" he asked whimsically. "We're engaged."

"Stop saying that! You never even asked me to marry you!"

"I thought you were asking me."

"And you're agreeing, is that it?" she whispered in a distant tone.

"Yes."

So simple, so unmistakably plain. He was agreeing to her price. Adena bit her lip as she sank back into the seat, stricken with a new thought. *Had* she unconsciously been asking him for marriage when she'd tossed away that so-casual line about being engaged? Her fingers curled into her palms as the car raced across the bridge.

"Please, Holt," she begged quietly. "I need time to think."

"You can think at home," he smiled, as if amused.

"*My* home."

"Our home," he corrected indulgently, taking the turnoff to Sausalito.

It was hopeless. "You...you can't kidnap me the way you did Max," Adena tried valiantly.

"I already have," he pointed out amicably, slowing the car gently for a turn and accelerating briefly as the Ferrari came out of it.

"We can pick up Max and then you can drive me back across the bridge," she declared regally.

The gold gleamed on his wrist as Holt deftly turned the wheel. He said nothing. Feeling quite helpless, Adena ran out of words as the Ferrari climbed the hillside street toward the modern structure Holt called home.

He continued to say nothing as he parked the car and politely opened the door. Adena stepped out uneasily, not knowing what to do. She felt terribly torn, terribly trapped by her feelings for this man.

It was Max who opened the next conversation, bouncing happily to greet them as the door opened. His short tail twitched with pleasure as he thrust his nose first against Adena's hand and then Holt's.

"I'm glad you're still up, Max," Holt remarked conversationally, closing the door. "You can join Adena and me in a glass of sherry. I had Annie buy some yesterday."

"You not only kidnap my dog, you try to corrupt him!" Adena complained, trailing slowly into the living room behind her captor as he found the sherry bottle and a couple of glasses.

"This is a celebration," Holt protested as he poured two glasses of sherry and put a drop or two into a saucer for Max. Max sniffed appreciatively. "Surely you want him to join in the congratulatory toast! Max, Adena and I are going to be married, aren't you pleased?''

Max ignored the question, removing the small amount of sherry from his plate with a polite swipe of his tongue.

''See? He's thrilled.'' Holt grinned, sinking down onto the couch and pulling Adena down beside him.

''Holt,'' Adena began determinedly, ''this is a very serious matter. We need to talk and I, for one, have got to have some time to think. I feel like everything's rushing along and I'm being swept into something that...''

He finished a sip of the sherry and set his glass down on the coffee table. There was a gray fire smoldering in his eyes as he drew her stiff body closer to his own.

''I haven't had time to thank you properly for my watch,'' he mused, studying her upturned, anxious features.

''It's all right, I mean, I...''

He kissed her floundering protest to a halt. ''It's the most fantastic watch I've ever seen,'' he growled against her lips. ''I still can't believe you gave it to me. No one's ever given me anything like it.''

''Oh, Holt,'' she sighed, collapsing into his arms under the impact of his gratitude and pleasure. ''Do you really like it that much?''

''Come here and I'll show you how much,'' he

murmured seductively, settling her lightly against his chest while his hands sought the delicate fastenings of her jewel-toned silk dress.

She trembled as his fingers lightly stroked the nape of her neck and then unfastened the bodice of the soft material. Closing her eyes on a wave of tenderness and love, Adena leaned her head against his shoulder and let him slip the silk from her shoulders. He wanted her and he was willing to marry her. It was as much as she could expect at this point from a man who didn't understand above love.

"Are you really going to marry me, Holt?" She could have bitten out her tongue at the words. They sounded as if she were verifying his agreement to her terms before surrendering to him.

"Yes," he rasped into her hair as he lowered the silk to her waist. "I'm going to marry you."

She heard Max abandon the hope of receiving any more sherry and flop down contentedly across the room. Her dog had certainly made himself at home, Adena thought vaguely as Holt's hands moved down the length of her naked back and then back up to find the catch which opened the scrap of lace that confined her small breasts. She shivered again when her bra was gently stripped from her and Holt touched the curving softness.

"I've been wanting you all evening," he grated huskily, letting his thumbs slowly circle her nipples in exciting, hypnotizing movements. "All through dinner, at the party, during the drive home tonight. I kept telling myself that the feeling was mutual. Every time I looked at the watch on my wrist, I told myself she really wants me too. She wouldn't have given me a gift like this if she didn't mean it."

Adena lifted her arms to encircle his neck. With her head tipped back, her wide turquoise eyes melded with his own gaze, and her lips quivered softly, as she faced him.

"I want you, Holt, but you don't have to marry me. Please, believe me, I never meant to force you into something like that."

"Force me? It's been a long time since I let anyone force me into doing anything, Adena West," he retorted half humorously.

"What I'm trying to say…" she began desperately.

"I know what you're trying to say, sweetheart, but it's too late. You've already made the commitment. You wouldn't back out of it now, would you?" He smiled wistfully. "Saying you'd changed your mind about marrying me would be like saying you wanted to take back the watch!"

Adena flinched, feeling the quicksand sucking her under again. "I wasn't going to take back the watch," she muttered guiltily.

"I know," he whispered. "And you won't

change your mind about marrying me, either, will you? I want you so much, Adena.''

''But, marriage…!'' she squeaked.

''Marriage is the only way you'll be able to convince yourself to come and live with me. I understand that. You'd be uncomfortable and restless in a long-term affair. You'd probably want to keep your own apartment.''

''Well, naturally!''

''And you'd worry about the future. No, I can understand that you want a formal commitment in exchange for giving yourself to me as completely as I need you to do. And I do need you, honey,'' he went on, bending his dark head to drop feathery kisses along the line of her throat just below her ear. ''I need to know you're mine and that you'll stay mine.''

Adena groaned, seeing no way out of the quagmire. He had talked himself into believing that marriage was the only way she would be able to surrender completely. He was more than willing to pay the price, and she could see no method of explaining herself.

Still, she had to make some attempt to control the situation for both their sakes. Holt was willing to rush into marriage because at the moment his desire for her was burning high. But how would he feel if he had time to think about what he was doing? Perhaps when the heat of his passion had cooled a little he would be content with an affair.

"I'll marry you, Holt," she breathed, clinging to him as he shaped the curve of her waist.

"I thought you would," he chuckled softly. "After the way you gave yourself to me last night and after your gift this morning..."

"But I think both of us need some time," she interrupted firmly as she toyed with the curling black hair on his neck. She felt him go quite still.

"How much time?"

"I don't know! A few weeks or months, perhaps. Holt, this is a very big move. We have to be sure..." She drew back a little to meet his slate-colored eyes and knew she had at last succeeded in getting him to take her seriously! A little too seriously, perhaps.

"And during those weeks or months you'll be living by yourself? Seeing me when it's convenient? Working me into your busy schedule?" he gritted, the brackets on either side of his mouth tightening ominously.

"We'll...we'll get to know each other. It will be a proper sort of engagement."

"No."

"No!" she exploded, pulling back even further. Hurriedly she picked up the silky material of her dress and held it in front of herself. "Now, Holt, you listen to me! I've had a very rough day as I keep trying to point out. I have just about reached my limit. You will not sit there and give me orders about the future direction of this—this *relationship!* I'm feeling a little confused at the moment," she went on grandly, "and I will not be talked into something that could complicate both our lives to no end just because your hormones and adrenalin are running high tonight!"

He smiled with sexy wickedness, reaching for her. "Come here, honey, and I'll see to it that your hormones and adrenalin catch up with mine."

"No! Damn it, Holt! I mean it! I won't be rushed into bed or marriage or anything else until we have a clear understanding of what's going on here!"

"Hush, darling," he placated, getting to his feet and swinging her lightly up into his arms. "You've admitted you're a little confused tonight, but I'm functioning just fine. Relax, and I'll make the decisions for both of us."

"The hell you will! Put me down, Holt!"

"Not until I've thanked you for the watch."

He was striding down a honey beige hall which was lined with mirrors from floor to ceiling on one side. Adena had a glimpse of herself lying half-naked in his arms, her dress draped wantonly around her waist, and one evening sandal missing from a shapely foot.

Holt moved with the easy power and grace of a

conqueror on his way to master the reluctant slave girl in his arms. It was all so primitive and so compelling that Adena felt a wave of sheer panic rise up and threaten to crash around her.

He carried her into the bedroom, setting her lightly down on the red and gold spread of a black lacquered bed. Adena glanced around in a daze as she struggled to a sitting position and pushed the hair out of her eyes. As with the rest of the house the striking red and black furniture was kept from being too dark by a gold and beige color on the floor and on the walls. But the heavy masculinity of the room oppressed her, inundating her with a sense of inevitability.

"Stop looking so edgy, honey," Holt murmured as he began to unbutton his shirt. "Everything's going to be all right. You want me and I want you. What could be simpler? I've told you I'll give you whatever you want, and tonight you made it pretty clear you want marriage. If marriage will make it easier for you to be my woman, then that's what you'll have."

"You make it sound as if I'm selling myself to you, Holt!" she cried angrily as the white shirt fell to the floor and he went to work on the buckle of his slacks.

"Stop putting words in my mouth. I never said that. Haven't I just told you that marriage suits me, too?" He stepped out of his slacks and stood beside the bed clothed only in a pair of white jockey shorts. His gray eyes raked her hungrily. "Adena, honey, don't deny me tonight. I need you."

She looked up at him, trying to find the willpower to refuse him. It was impossible. His gray eyes were glowing with a need she couldn't bring herself to squash, just as she hadn't been able to tell him the real reason she'd given him the watch. Perhaps this was the way it was with love, she thought wonderingly.

"Would you go away tonight if I sent you?" she asked very quietly.

He hesitated. She could see him grappling with the unexpected question and she couldn't bear the hurt in him. It was as if she'd hurt herself.

"Oh, Holt," she breathed, lifting a hand to catch one of his. "You idiot. You must know I'd never send you away."

The misty gaze cleared instantly and she saw the relief in him. He came down beside her on the red and gold spread and gathered her into his arms.

"I don't ever want to hear that question again," he rasped thickly as he slipped the silk dress off her completely. "Adena, I want to be married at the end of the week. We can go to Reno."

"The end of the week! But, Holt, why so soon?"

"So you can't ask me a question like that again," he growled.

"I won't ask again," she promised, pressing her lips against his chest as he ran a hand along the curve of her hip. She was trembling already as he slowly stoked the fires of her desire.

"No," he agreed in satisfaction. "As my wife, you can't turn me away!"

"You have a very old-fashioned view of marriage," she teased shakily, running her fingertip down to the masculine nipple and glorying in the instant response of his body.

"I'm glad you realize that," he told her fervently, nuzzling under the curve of her hair to find the sensitive skin of her shoulder.

"Especially considering the fact that up until a very short while ago, you didn't even know you were getting married," Adena concluded dryly.

"As soon as you opened your mouth tonight at the party, I saw it was the perfect solution. You'll have what you want and I'll have what I want." He bit very gently into the curve of her shoulder as his fingers flattened possessively across her stomach.

"I thought you were content with what you had last night," she whispered breathlessly as the hand on her stomach moved lower.

"I want you in a position where you can't reject my gifts or me," he muttered as he began to draw lazy kisses across her breasts. "I want you to feel comfortable in taking what I have to offer so you won't throw my presents back in my face. As my wife you won't have any qualms about accepting what I can give you. And you'll belong to me completely."

"You think that's a fair exchange?" Her body arched helplessly against his questing fingers and Holt smiled with a sensual satisfaction.

"Oh, yes, it's a fair exchange!"

But for how long would he consider it so? Adena wondered dimly as the waves of seductive sensation washed over her. How would Holt seek to pay off a wife he wanted out of his life?

The painful thought was pushed forcibly to the back of her mind as Adena came to tingling awareness beneath his touch. She would worry about reality later. Tonight Holt was offering magic, and she silently endowed it with her own very private love for him. The combination was irresistible.

With a soft moan, Adena curled her fingers into the darkness of his hair and guided his face down to her waiting mouth.

"Adena…!"

Gently he crushed her beneath him as the kiss deepened. She felt him exploring her body while his tongue explored the sweetness of her mouth, and with undisguised passion she yielded him the territory he sought.

When he tangled his fist in her hair, Adena realized he hadn't removed the watch. It gleamed in the dim light, a symbol of his commitment to her. A very expensive symbol, she reflected a bit wryly. But she knew him well enough now to know he wouldn't have accepted the gift if he hadn't wanted her. He was an honest man.

At that moment Adena knew she would give him anything he asked of her. She would see to it that Holt Sinclair received full value in a wife. More value than he even knew.

But that was all right. She would give the gift of her love silently, but she would give it completely. And someday he would realize there was something more he had to give her, something she longed for far more than golden necklaces and promises of marriage. Holt Sinclair could be taught to love. She would be his teacher.

Satisfied with her decision, Adena toyed lightly with the crisp hairs on his arm, following the feel of them up to where the gold watch circled his wrist.

"Beautiful, isn't it?" he drawled huskily as he realized what she was doing. "Like the woman who gave it to me."

Adena smiled invitingly up at him. "The necklace you gave me this morning is lovely, too, Holt. I'm sorry I lost my temper over it. I thought...I thought..."

"I know what you thought," he said quietly. "Just remember I never give anything I don't want to give. Consider it my engagement present to you," he added on a throaty laugh.

His engagement present. Yes, she thought bravely, that's how she would view the gold and diamond necklace. She could hardly refuse to wear his gift after witnessing Holt's unaffected pleasure in hers.

The rippling tide began tugging at her body, arousing the erotic tension below her stomach and making her conscious of the tightness of her swollen breasts. He had such power over her, she thought briefly while she still could think at all. A power unlike any other man. Or did loving someone put you under his spell this thoroughly?

"Let me hear you say how much you want me," Holt coaxed, tracing persuasive little patterns up the inside of her thighs while his tongue moved sensuously on her nipple. "Tell me why you gave me the watch."

For an instant Adena stiffened and then she realized he wasn't looking for any other reason for her gift than the one he'd already invented. He just wanted to hear her confirm it again because it was another way of confessing her desire.

"I want you, Holt. You make my body sing and you set my blood on fire. I shouldn't let you do this to me but I don't think I could refuse you even if you refused to marry me!"

"Good," he told her in a deep voice laced with evident satisfaction. "That's the way it should be. Because you do the same thing to me, sweetheart, and I couldn't refuse you anything either. Marriage is a small price to pay for owning you completely. Hell, I would have given you the world!"

A small price to pay for owning her. Adena repeated the words to herself but she couldn't seem to focus on them at that moment. He was assaulting her with a tender strength that made it impossible to concentrate on anything else in the world except him.

Deliberately he set one knee between her thighs and pressed until she shifted her legs to allow him close to her body. He sank down into her warmth as if he were losing himself in her embrace.

"Hold me," he growled fiercely as he mastered her body with heat and power. "Hold me as if you'll never let go!"

Adena clung to him, her senses spinning as he made them into one entity for a timeless interval that went beyond any gift of gold.

Nine

Adena woke next morning at the gentle urging of a friendly, but cold, gray nose. There was no moment of disorientation. As soon as her eyes opened, she knew exactly where she was.

Max's hopeful eyes met hers as she peered over the edge of the bed and Adena smiled slightly. It was time for the dog's morning walk, and some routines mustn't be broken.

Carefully she pushed aside the covers, aware of Holt's gloriously naked form sprawled beside her. There was no need to wake him, she decided magnanimously. But for a moment she gazed down at the lean, tanned body so close to hers.

His near-black hair was tousled rakishly and the white sheet only covered him to the waist. He lay on his stomach and the sight of his sinewy, muscled back brought back thoughts that made Adena's cheeks turn warm. There was a physical as well as a non-physical power in him that she had been made to know well last night.

Her body protested mildly as she sat up and slid quietly out of bed. Her own gentler muscles seemed to have a vivid memory of the impact Holt's had made on hers, she thought wryly. It was as if he had been determined to imprint himself on her. Over and over again he had wrapped her tightly in the folds of his passion and carried her out into the depths where she had to cling to him for safety.

Always well-mannered, Max waited with polite eagerness as Adena searched for something to wear outside. The silk dress wasn't going to offer much protection against the cold, foggy morning but Adena slipped it on and then padded out of the bedroom, her evening shoes in her hand. Max followed jauntily.

In a hall closet Adena finally found what she needed, a man's suede coat with a thick sheepskin lining. It fell almost to her knees as she fastened it about her, and the weight of it was another reminder of the more intimate weight of its owner.

"All right," she whispered to Max as she let them

both stealthily out the kitchen door, "you're on your own this morning. I don't know where your leash is and I don't feel like looking for little plastic bags in Annie's kitchen. Try to be discreet, will you?"

Max raced off delightedly, happy to be free of the familiar leash. There was a great deal of genuine open space around and the thrill of exploration away from the usual sidewalk environment lent an extra bounce to his stride. Adena followed more slowly, huddled into the depths of the sheepskin coat. She hoped none of the neighbors would be up at this early hour on a Saturday morning. It might take some doing trying to explain a pair of evening shoes and an outsized man's coat.

The chill of the morning gradually cleared her sleepy thoughts and she looked out across the Bay to the sight of fog-shrouded San Francisco. She should have been waking up there this morning, she thought grimly. Spending the night in Holt Sinclair's bed set a dangerous precedent and she knew it.

Dazedly she tried to sort out the confused conversation of the evening. Adena had the distinct sensation she'd been maneuvered very neatly, not only into bed, but into an engagement. Why had she had all that champagne on top of the wine at dinner?

But there was no use dwelling on the past. She had been driven by a combination of circumstances and the force of her new-found love into a very untenable situation.

Oh, she wanted to marry Holt, Adena didn't bother to deny that to herself. But not like this! Not when he'd convinced himself it was her price!

She watched Max sniffing about among a clump of trees and wondered what she was going to say over breakfast. There was no doubt that Holt would assume everything had been settled last night. She knew from the possessive, masterful way in which he'd made love to her that he was staking a claim.

The awkward part was that she really didn't want to deny the claim, wasn't certain she could. But Adena knew she definitely did not want him marrying her just because he was trying to meet her price!

"Come on, Max, let's go!" she called softly. "My feet are getting cold!"

Reluctantly the schnauzer trotted toward her, pausing occasionally for last-minute inspections of interesting points along the way. Adena reached down to pat him affectionately as he reached her, and they both turned to start back toward the house.

It was Max who spotted Holt standing beside the Ferrari, keys in his hand. The dog bounded forward with a small, cheerful yip of pleasure and Holt's hand fell slowly away from the car door to stroke the dog's ears.

But his narrowed gray eyes met Adena's with an

enigmatic pain that made her falter briefly before she continued on up the driveway. At least, she thought it had been pain, but as she approached him, the look faded first to something that might have been overwhelming relief and then to something harder.

Unable to comprehend the intensity of his expression as Holt watched her come toward him, Adena said nothing. When she stood only a couple of feet away he reached out and circled her nape with the palm of his hand.

"I thought you and Max had left," he said simply in a strangely neutral voice that alarmed her.

Adena tried to smile, conscious of the hard urgency in him. She glanced meaningfully at the car and the keys in his hand. "Were you going to come after us?" she demanded lightly.

He nodded, his jaw set grimly. "I was going to bring you home."

Adena met his hooded gaze with a bland cheeriness she was far from feeling. "Max and I," she confided, "would never leave before breakfast."

For an instant longer Holt raked her face, and then some of the tautness in him relaxed. "I'll remember that."

He took her hand without another word and started back toward the front door.

Half an hour later Adena covered the poached eggs with hollandaise sauce and carried the tray of eggs Benedict over to the kitchen table where Holt was lazily flipping through the morning paper. She poured another cup of tea for him, waited until he'd set down the paper and examined his breakfast appreciatively, and then decided to take her stand.

"About going home," she began staunchly as he forked up a large bite.

One sable brow lifted quizzically as he chewed. "Hmmmm?"

"I don't know exactly what happened last night," Adena continued forcefully and pointedly ignored the hint of wicked laughter in his misty eyes, which now met hers with a familiar indulgence. "But I want to make it perfectly clear that I'm not moving in with you, Holt. Furthermore, if you're serious about getting married..."

"I am," he interrupted briefly.

"Then I've decided we're going to have a proper engagement. We're not going to rush into this. Also," she went on quickly, "I don't want our judgment to be clouded by...by..."

"Sex?" he suggested helpfully, cutting another bite of eggs with his fork.

"Exactly! I'm glad you understand," she exclaimed in surprised relief.

He chewed thoughtfully for a moment, eyeing her interestedly. "Would it help if I assured you my judgment isn't clouded at all? That I know exactly what I want?"

"No."

"You don't believe me?" he asked reproachfully.

"I believe you're willing to pay for what you want in life, Holt," she replied steadily, knowing she had to stick by her guns this morning. "And, as you've told me many times, you're a generous man."

"Adena," he began quietly, his gray eyes darkening slightly.

But she put up a hand to ward off his next words. "I mean it, Holt. Last night everything was confused and out of control. But this morning..."

"This morning you've reasoned everything out, is that it?" he drawled.

"Holt, I want your word that you will respect my wishes in this matter," she declared very formally, chin lifted challengingly.

He waited for a moment before replying, and Adena felt the tension crackle in the air between them. "Let me get this perfectly straight," he finally murmured. "You want a platonic engagement with no major seduction scenes. At the end of said engagement you will then marry me as promised last night."

She nodded stiffly. "If you still want to marry me

after the engagement is over," she hedged deliberately.

"I'm not likely to change my mind in a week."

"A week!"

"I said last night we would be married next weekend," he reminded her.

"But, Holt, that's hardly long enough to find out if we're truly suited!" she protested. Hardly long enough, she added in silent anguish, to determine if you really can learn to love me!

He considered her worried expression for a few seconds. "For the whole of this week," he vowed softly, "I won't lay a hand on you."

"Two weeks," she tried desperately.

"It seems to me that you're bargaining abilities are improving rapidly," he noted coolly. "All right. Two weeks."

God! He thought she was dealing again! But there was no help for it. They needed time, both of them, and Adena didn't know how else to buy it.

"Thank you, Holt," she said quietly.

He waved off her stiff gratitude. "As you said, I'm a generous man." But the hard light in his eyes was anything but generous and Adena was well aware of it.

Nevertheless, he was as good as his word. The remainder of the weekend went by in a surprisingly pleasant round of small adventures. They went shopping in the charming boutiques along the Sausalito waterfront, walked through Muir Woods, the five hundred and two acre national monument named for the famous naturalist John Muir and had lunch at Fisherman's Wharf in San Francisco.

Saturday and Sunday night he took her gallantly back to her apartment, poured himself a glass of sherry, and eventually left her with only a good-night kiss.

By Wednesday a reasonably amicable routine seemed to have established itself. Holt had taken to showing up on her doorstep for dinner and making himself at home. After the meal Adena would find herself sitting beside him in front of the fire, casually working her crewel embroidery while she talked to him about everything from the day's events to which was the best Japanese restaurant in the city. Max dozed contentedly at their feet and Adena would tell herself from time to time that the domesticity seemed out of character for Holt.

Or was it a side of his character he simply hadn't had an opportunity to indulge until now? Adena was wondering about the sort of life-style Holt must have enjoyed in the past as she sat stitching a flower on Wednesday night when he surprised her by asking calmly, "Have you accepted the accounting position you interviewed for on Friday?"

She started, fumbling the complicated stitch she

had been making, and glanced up to find him watching her lazily.

"No," she admitted coolly, bending her head to continue her work.

"Are you going to accept it?" he pressed softly.

"No."

"Why not, Adena?"

"You know the answer to that," she said calmly, but her fingers trembled slightly.

"If I hadn't been involved, you would have joined the company, wouldn't you?" he probed.

"Yes."

He leaned forward, forcing her chin up with his hand. "You are the most annoying, stubborn little wench I've ever met, do you realize that? Can't you learn to accept my gifts graciously? I want to do things for you, Adena. I want to give you things."

She met his eyes and for an instant her blue and green gaze clashed with his steel gray one. "I know you do, Holt, but it's not necessary."

"You're afraid to accept anything from me, even marriage," he accused softly.

"You're so accustomed to buying everything. You see life as a series of financial transactions. It frightens me a little."

"How do I frighten you?" he demanded, his eyes never leaving hers.

She lifted one shoulder in a small shrug. How

could she explain? "I suppose, partly at least, because I'm afraid of what would happen if you decided you weren't getting full value."

He watched her for a moment longer and then he released her chin and lounged back into the corner of the sofa. The enigmatic, assessing gleam had returned to his gray eyes. "Are you thinking of shortchanging me?" he asked blandly.

"What would you do if you felt shortchanged?" she whispered, her hands still on the embroidery frame. Adena experienced a definite chill down the length of her spine as he regarded her broodingly.

His mouth tightened. "If I thought you were cheating me," he began remotely. "I wouldn't be responsible for anything I might do."

"You'd be furious," she sighed, desperately forcing a smile as she picked up her embroidery again. "I thought so! And you ask me why I'm frightened!"

There was a moment of very tense silence and then Holt smiled a little dangerously. "This is, I take it, a strictly hypothetical discussion?"

"Strictly," she assured him with a lightness she was far from feeling.

"In the case, I suggest we abandon it. Hypothetical discussions seldom resolve anything useful."

"Whatever you say," she agreed calmly. But when she looked down at the design on the green fabric her mind saw not the exotic flower taking shape under her fingers, but the image of a man who could never fully trust anyone because he was of the opinion that anyone could be bought. Could such a man ever learn to love?

The call from Holt's secretary came around eleven o'clock on Thursday morning. It was an unfamiliar voice, but Adena assumed a man in Holt's position had more than one secretary.

"Miss West?" began the formal tones on the other end of the line.

"Yes," Adena agreed pleasantly, cradling the phone against her shoulder as she licked an envelope which was about to go out with another résumé.

"I'm calling for Mr. Sinclair. He would like to know if you can join him for lunch with a client this afternoon."

"Why, yes, I suppose so." Vaguely surprised at the request but delighted, nevertheless, Adena quickly jotted down the name of a restaurant near Holt's office and repeated the instructions to meet him in the lobby.

"He'll have a Mr. Rawlins with him," the woman concluded briskly.

"Thank you. Tell Holt I'll be there." She'd met John Rawlins the night of the party, Adena reflected as she concluded her résumé work and went in search of a proper little suit for a business lunch.

Was Holt going to be the kind of husband who liked his wife to help entertain clients?

Half an hour later, chicly attired in a conservative skirt and jacket done in a soft, expensive wool, Adena bid farewell to Max and headed for the bus downtown. There was no point trying to drive in the city during the day, not when public transportation was more than adequate.

She knew the popular executive luncheon spot Holt had selected. With its austerely dressed waiters, formal white tablecloths and old-fashioned Victorian ambience, it had the atmosphere of a staid men's club. But the food, Adena thought with relish, was excellent.

There was no need to hurry, she was going to be a few minutes early as it was. Adena swung gracefully into the waiting area near the restaurant lounge, glanced around automatically, and nearly collided with an all-too-familiar figure.

"Adena!"

"Jeff! What are you doing here?" Instinctively she put her hands up to steady herself and he caught one lightly.

"I've just finished lunch, naturally." He smiled with the same boyish expression she had once found so attractive. "How about you? Meeting someone?"

"Well, yes, as a matter of fact, I am," she replied, feeling a little awkward.

"Let me guess." Jeff's mouth twisted ruefully. "Holt Sinclair?"

"I'm afraid so." Hastily she straightened herself and stepped back, uncertain of his mood.

"Don't worry," Jeff Carrigan groaned, seeing her wary look. "I'm my normal self. I guess I should apologize about the other evening." He lifted one hand in which he held a long white envelope and dropped it again. "All I can say is, I'd had a couple of drinks and I'd just lost a very important woman in my life to an arch rival."

"Jeff, please don't talk about it," Adena begged, horribly embarrassed. "I'm just as sorry about the whole mess as you are. It's one of those things that's better forgotten."

"I don't mind forgetting the incident, but it's going to take a while to forget you, Adena," he murmured deeply, taking a step closer.

A potted palm blocked any retreat she might have made, so Adena stood her ground and smiled bravely. "Please, Jeff…"

He stopped, smiling sadly. "I really blew it with you, didn't I?"

"I…I think it was all wrong in the first place, Jeff," she whispered unhappily, wishing the uncomfortable little scene would end quickly. She wasn't looking forward to having Holt interrupt it!

"No, but I freely admit I handled it all wrong. We had a lot in common, Adena, didn't we?"

"Well, yes, perhaps, but..." Good grief? How did a woman get rid of an ex-boyfriend who wanted to stand around and reminisce?

"Remember how we used to come here occasionally for lunch? I'm going to miss those lunches," he persisted relentlessly.

Adena became belatedly aware of a certain iciness under his outwardly rueful exterior.

"I'd rather not talk about it, Jeff..."

"I'm sure you wouldn't." He covered the hint of resentment in his voice with a smile and repeated his statement. "No, I'm sure you wouldn't want to talk about us. You've landed very nicely on your feet, haven't you?"

"That's enough, Jeff. If you'll excuse me, I'll..."

"Doesn't the ex get a farewell kiss?" he murmured, closing the small distance between them.

Adena realized she was literally trapped by the palm. Anger began to replace embarrassment and her eyes narrowed warningly. "Good-bye, Jeff."

"Good-bye, Adena," he said very coolly but with a warm smile that belied the repressed fury in his eyes. Fury and a curious satisfaction that Adena saw too late.

Before she could slip aside, he had caught her by the shoulders in a bruising grip. He tugged her close, kissed her roughly on the mouth as she gasped, and then released her before she could verbalize a protest.

"Thanks for everything, darling," he drawled and shoved the white envelope into her hand.

Her fingers closed around the envelope automatically as Adena glared up into his handsome, smiling features. But before she could think of sufficiently condemning words, Jeff was gone, striding briskly past her toward the door.

She swung around to watch him leave, disgusted with herself for having gotten into the awkward situation. There was no point making a scene now, she thought grimly as Jeff strode past the two men who had just entered the restaurant and who must have seen the kiss.

Adena was so occupied glaring after Jeff that she didn't pay any attention to the two witnesses until she saw Jeff nod coolly at one before letting himself out the door.

Holt. Beside him stood John Rawlins.

Adena could have screamed in frustration as she realized what Jeff had just done to her. Her appalled gaze clashed and clung to the cold steel in her lover's eyes and she wanted to run. Run as she had never run before in her life.

The she remembered the white envelope in her hand. Slowly it began to dawn on her just how extensive Jeff's revenge might have been. Surely he wouldn't have been so cruel as to compromise her completely in Holt's eyes...?

But she knew the answer to that even as Holt started forward. Helplessly she waited for him, unable even to begin thinking of a rational explanation that might pacify him. The envelope in her hand doomed her. She knew it with a sense of total, bleak inevitability.

He came toward her, dark and sleek and dangerous in the dim light of the restaurant lobby. John Rawlins trailed weakly behind, uncertain of what was happening.

Without a word, Holt came to a stop in front of her and held out his hand. His eyes raked her taut features as she slowly handed over the damning envelope.

He was all steel and contained menace, she thought dazedly as she watched him slit the envelope and lift out the folded piece of paper inside. She knew a fear she had never known before as he silently scanned the handwriting Adena knew must be Jeff's.

When he'd finished, he shook something else out of the envelope—a check. Adena flinched as she saw it fall into his hand.

Holt glance disdainfully at the amount and then handed both the paper and the check over to Adena.

She accepted them with shaky fingers, aware of the fear which had set her heart racing. Unable to do anything else she read the brief note from Jeff.

Keep up the good work, sweetheart. We'll be married when it's all over, she read. The check, signed by Jeff, was for several hundred dollars.

Mutely Adena lifted her eyes from the evidence against her and awaited Holt's verdict. There was nothing she could say and she knew it. Holt, who firmly believed everyone had a price, would think that Jeff had been paying hers all along. He would believe exactly what Jeff wanted him to believe: that Adena had been assigned to seduce Carrigan Labs' arch rival.

"Excuse us, John. I'll be right back," Holt said quietly to the other man who hovered in the background. He took Adena's arm in a grip of iron and walked her to the front door. She felt as if she were being led to the scaffold.

But whatever Holt thought, she reminded herself harshly, she was innocent. Unconsciously her head came up proudly.

Out on the busy sidewalk, Holt flagged a taxi and opened the door for her as it slowed.

"Go home," he instructed in a deadly soft voice as she slid down onto the seat. He shut the door and leaned over to pin her through the window with an expression that was as chilling as the North Sea.

"I'll be there in a couple of hours. There are one or two things I have to take care of first. And don't look so frightened, Adena, I won't use my fists. I'm capable of exacting a more subtle revenge than that!"

Ten

A more subtle revenge.

Three times during the course of that long afternoon Adena hesitated in front of the closet, wondering if the smartest thing to do was pull down the
suitcase, put Max in the car, and leave.

But she was innocent, damn it! Every time that
thought crossed her mind, the memory of Jeff's
treachery returned and with it the image of Holt's
haunting fury.

Because he had been furious. There was no doubt
about it. The cold mist in his fog-gray eyes had
seemed to contain a controlled anger that was far
more menacing than outright, red-hot fury would
have been.

How could she ever explain what Holt had seen in that restaurant? Again and again Adena asked herself that, going over and over a series of explanations that always seemed to fall flat when she practiced them aloud.

Max watched worriedly from his place behind the couch. Chin resting on his paws, his gaze followed Adena as she stalked back and forth across the persimmon carpet.

"Will you defend me this time?" Adena stopped to ask with a rueful smile as she reached down and gently stroked his back. "If I sicked you on Holt would you treat him the way you treated Jeff?"

Max stared back mutely and Adena rose to walk over to the sherry table. She eyed the crystal decanter for a moment, remembering how many times Holt had helped himself to the amber liquid inside. He'd enjoyed making himself at home in her apartment.

Adena turned away from the sherry. She was going to need all her wits about her when Holt showed up on her doorstep. She would have to make him listen to her, that was all there was to it!

The urgency of that thought made her pause again. The logical thing to do was to tell him her side of the story, and if he refused to believe her, tell him to go to hell!

She had her pride, didn't she? It would be his own

fault if his philosophy of life blinded him from seeing the truth in this situation.

Even as she gave herself the admonition, however, another truth intruded. She loved him. It wasn't simply a matter of pride that he believe her, it was imperative! More than anything else on earth, Adena knew, she wanted Holt's trust.

Because trust was a major stepping stone to love. If she had that... Adena took a deep breath. Somehow she had to convince him of her innocence.

But how could she go about convincing him, a man who thought anything and anyone could be bought, that she was not deceiving him? Holt Sinclair was a very practical man, as he'd pointed out on more than one occasion. He accepted all too readily the notion that everything had to be paid for in life and he was more than willing to pay for what he took.

And he'd also hinted more than once that he expected full value in exchange for his generosity. Adena bit her lip as she stood in front of the bay window overlooking the street. One did not cheat a man like Holt Sinclair and come away unscathed.

What was he doing now? Had he gone politely ahead with the client luncheon? Business first and then revenge? The thought of such calculating coldness made her wince.

What would it take to make a man like Holt trust

a woman? Was it even possible? But if it were, Adena knew it would mean almost as much to her as an open admission of his love.

She could hardly expect trust in a situation such as this, though, she told herself in disgust as she paced back across the room. The evidence was too damning. Jeff had taken his revenge very thoroughly.

Adena looked again at the sherry. She needed something for her jangled nerves. Then, with grim resolution, she headed for the kitchen and carefully made herself a pot of Darjeeling tea. The ritual, itself, helped steady her, she realized.

By the time the tea had steeped and Adena had gotten out a cup and saucer, she had decided upon her approach to the disaster. Carrying the tea out into the living room, and sitting down on the green and persimmon print chair, she sipped deliberately as she thought. She would be cool and poised and regal. She would not allow Holt to send her into a panic. After all, she was innocent! Eventually, perhaps, when his anger had receded, she would be able to begin the long road back to trust.

If Holt Sinclair ever could be taught to trust.

That thought brought on a new wave of depression which unfortunately coincided with the chiming of the doorbell. In spite of all her resolutions, Adena jumped, the cup rattling dangerously in the saucer.

Her palms dampened as she set down the tea and got to her feet. Max rose also, his short tail wagging enthusiastically. Clearly he didn't yet see the menace in the arrival of his friend.

It took a great deal of courage to walk to the door and put her hand on the knob. Never in her life had Adena felt so much like running in the opposite direction. The prospect of trying to explain the whole mess seemed suddenly, appallingly, impossible. How would she ever get Holt to believe her side?

But she had to make the attempt. She loved him too much not to make the effort to try to salvage the relationship. Perhaps she would be able to weather the storm of his fury and, when it was over, begin rebuilding the fragile web of desire and affection he'd felt for her.

Far more likely, she told herself bitterly, he would simply walk out of her life after exacting his "revenge." She opened the door.

He stood there, lending as always a satisfyingly dark and solid presence to the light, feminine room. Adena stared up at him for a long instant, cataloging the taut line of his mouth, the appraisal in his cool, gray eyes, and the hard leanness of him. It was hopeless. What had ever made her think she could eventually make him trust her? Every inch, every sinew, every fiber of Holt Sinclair was conditioned to see the actions of others in terms of buying and selling. And he would be feeling cheated at the moment.

Her hand still on the doorknob, Max prancing far too cheerfully at her feet, Adena lifted her face defiantly. A rush of righteous indignation went through her, momentarily replacing her fear.

"I didn't do it," she declared starkly. "I wasn't working for Jeff Carrigan or his firm!"

He looked at her, his dark lashes lowering in lazy consideration of her tension-sharpened face.

"I know that," he announced with such unruffled calm that Adena fell back a step in astonishment.

He pushed gently past her, patted Max affectionately, and headed for the sherry table. Adena watched in amazement as he casually poured himself a glass and turned to face her.

"Don't you think I know a setup when I see it?"

Clinging to the doorknob for support, Adena slowly shut the door, bracing herself against it with hands which trembled behind her back.

"You don't believe I was...was some sort of company spy for Carrigan Labs?" she managed. Her lips felt suddenly dry as she tried to absorb the shock.

Holt's mouth was edged in mild amusement as he lowered himself onto the sofa with the air of a man intent on enjoying some well-deserved relaxation. Eyes closed, he leaned back into the corner, one leg carelessly lying along the cushions. Slowly he sipped his sherry.

"Don't be ridiculous. Why on earth should I think that? I know you very well, Adena West, and just between the two of us, you'd make a lousy company spy. Not that you can't be charmingly seductive under the proper conditions," he went on meditatively, "but you don't really have the straightforward, mercenary inclination it takes to... Hey! What the...?"

Adena had practically flown across the room, hurling herself into his arms with an awkward impact that sent the sherry in his glass dangerously near the rim.

"You love me! You love me! Say it, Holt, please say it!"

Carefully he set the sherry glass down on the coffee table, straightening slowly as she clung to him around the waist, her face buried against his jacket.

"Adena, my darling, I think I fell in love with you that first night when you came to tell me about the payoffs Carrigan was making to one of my men," he rasped thickly, his hands tangling in her hair. There was a kind of wonder in his voice. "Don't tell me you just this instant realized it!"

"Yes, just this instant. I didn't dare to dream..."

"And what brought about this great revelation?" he mused. She could feel the tension in him now as he wrapped her closer against him and settled back again into the cushions.

"Only a man in love could have looked at that check and that note and that kiss in the restaurant and believed me innocent!" she breathed, lifting her face to meet his warmly intent gaze.

"A man in love who also happened to know his woman cared far too much for him to deceive him with another man," Holt amended gently, his fingers stroking back the curve of her hair as she lay cradled in his arms.

"Are you telling me you knew I loved you all along?"

"Do you love me, Adena?" he asked throatily. She could still sense the tension in his body.

"Yes," she answered simply. "Oh, yes, Holt. I love you." Her turquoise eyes glowed luminously with the warmth of her answer and Holt hugged her fiercely closer. Some of the tautness in him seemed to relax.

"I thought," he growled with soft humor, "that there might be hope in that direction when you couldn't bring yourself to demand that I return my beautiful watch!"

"What?" Startled at the implication of his words, Adena lifted her head away from his shoulder. "What are you talking about, Holt Sinclair?"

"I knew why you gave me the watch," he murmured, pulling her head lovingly back down on his shoulder. "You had it sent in a fit of rage after you found out I'd gotten you that interview, didn't you? I can see you now, marching into one of the most expensive jewelry shops in town and ordering that watch sent to me. The package was still tingling with the vibrations of outraged femininity when it arrived on my desk, I swear it!"

"I don't believe it!" she gasped. "You *knew?* You knew all along?"

"I'm afraid so. I spent the whole afternoon trying to figure out how to handle the situation. I realized I'd unintentionally offended you not once, but twice that day and you were trying to teach me a lesson."

"So you pretended to take my gift at face value!" she groaned ruefully. "You are a sneaky, conniving devil, Holt Sinclair, and if I didn't love you so much I would demand that watch back right now! What made you think I wouldn't at the time?" she thought to ask.

"I took a risk," he admitted with a reminiscent smile. "I took a chance that you wouldn't have the heart to hurt me if you thought I was genuinely enchanted with the gift. I knew from the way you'd given yourself to me the night before that you must have felt something real and important. You're too honest a woman to have surrendered the way you did in my arms otherwise. You can't fake that kind of warmth, honey.''

"You took advantage of my good nature!" she protested, a smile tugging at her lips even as she tried for a severe expression.

"I was desperate," he defended himself, his own mouth quirking upward as he watched her. "I knew you were trying to teach me a lesson. You thought I'd arrive in a fury, didn't you? You were going to let me accuse you of all sorts of nasty things…''

"I thought your pride would take the same blow mine took when I saw the necklace," Adena said quietly, her eyes sobering as she remembered that wretched morning. "I wanted you to see what it felt like to be *paid* for services rendered!''

"I knew it," he groaned ruefully. "And if it's any consolation to you, honey, I realized what you were trying to tell me the minute I opened the package. I saw at once how my necklace must have looked to you. When I realized you'd found out I'd also assisted in getting you that interview I knew I was in dire straits!''

"I like that!" she complained indignantly. "The least you could have done was give me the satisfaction of knowing I'd taught you a lesson!''

"I thought about that," he sighed. "I seriously considered playing out the insulted male scene and then going on to play the humble penitent, but it occurred to me I could avoid all the fireworks and perhaps find out exactly how you felt about me if I simply accepted your very generous present.''

She eyed him with a slanting glance. ''You must have had a good laugh over my reaction.''

''No,'' he assured her at once, sliding a hand up to the hollow of her throat in a slow caress. ''When you couldn't bring yourself to demand that the watch be returned, I knew I'd just received my real present. And I knew I couldn't have bought that kind of gift with all the necklaces in the world. I really will treasure my watch, sweetheart, because it symbolizes the moment I began to think you might come to love me.''

''You were so sure of me?'' she asked wistfully.

He grinned, a slashing, wicked grin that told her just how much he had learned about human nature in the course of what had been a rough life.

''Let's just say I was sure that no out-of-work accountant was going to spend that kind of money on revenge and then kiss it good-bye when the revenge failed to materialize unless she was caught up in some fairly deep emotion.''

Adena wrapped her arms around his neck, resigning herself to the inevitable. ''Well? Don't stop there! Tell me what went through your head when I made my grand announcement at the party that night!''

"When you told everyone the watch was an engagement present? What do you think went through my head? The opportunity was too good to miss. I just kept up the pressure until you found yourself agreeing to marry me." He looked enormously satisfied with himself.

"Anyone would think," she grumbled, "that it was all your idea!"

"Anyone would be right," he shrugged modestly. "Can I help it if I happen to have a talent for taking advantage of optimal situations?"

"I suppose you're going to keep the watch?"

"Naturally," he chuckled, lifting aside the curve of her umber hair to place a small, sizzling little kiss on her throat. "It's a sign of your commitment to me. But if you need money to cover the check you wrote for it, I'll be happy to..."

"No." She shushed him by placing her fingers firmly against his lips. "No, the gift is mine and I've already covered the check, although I'll admit I had a few bad moments figuring out how I was going to do it!"

"Is that why you were going through the wine and the champagne at such a rapid rate that night?" he teased, twining his hand in her hair as if the soft tresses were silk.

"You noticed!" she muttered.

"Everything did seem to be working in my favor

that evening," he observed pleasantly. "You were nicely confused and slightly off balance all during dinner and afterward."

"You mean you took advantage of me!" she accused, eyes gleaming.

"And how," he confirmed complacently.

She decided not to pursue that avenue of argument. He obviously had no qualms about what he'd done. "So you're going to let me buy you with a gold watch and a couple of nights of passion, hmmm?"

"For you the price will always be a special rate," he promised.

"I don't know how many Swiss watches I can afford," she warned.

"The price is love, sweetheart, not endless gold watches. Just give me all your love and passion and loyalty. You'll find me an honest businessman."

"I'll get full value for my investments?" she asked, running her fingertips through the hair on the back of his neck which intrigued her so.

"I'm loyal, good-tempered, devoted and house-broken."

"Just like Max," she noted happily.

"Ummm."

"I wasn't so certain about the good-tempered bit earlier today," she allowed quietly. "When you put me in that cab and talked about revenge..."

The sensuous humor in him vanished. "How could you have thought for one moment I meant revenge against you? I intended to straighten out Carrigan! My God! If I'd realized you thought I was going to come back here and...!" He broke off on a low growl of dismay. "Adena, I would never hurt you!"

"Even if you thought I'd cheated you?" she dared.

"You wouldn't ever do that and I seem to recall telling you once before that hypothetical discussions are fruitless. Let's talk about something else."

"Such as?"

"Such as where we're going to spend our honeymoon."

"There's something I'd rather discuss first," she said very carefully.

"Where we're going to get married? I figure we can just run up to Reno and then..."

"I meant what did you do to Jeff?" The shark she'd seen swimming in the cold gray depths of his eyes earlier that day had been intent on some prey. If she hadn't been the victim, then that left only Jeff.

"Oh, him." There was a supreme disinterest in his voice.

"Yes, him. I want to know what you did to him, Holt," she said very steadily.

"Do you care?" There was an element of watchfulness in him now.

"Not particularly," she admitted. "But I am curious. After spending the past couple of hours wondering what awful things you had planned for me I'm interested in knowing what you did to the real culprit."

"I see. Well, after I'd cooled down a bit I took into consideration the fact that if it hadn't been for him I might never have met you."

Adena's brow lifted in surprise. "Very generous of you."

"I keep telling you I'm a generous man. And then I tracked him down in his office in Carrigan Labs and gave him to understand that if he came near you again I'd ruin his reputation and that of his father throughout the entire San Francisco business community."

She drew in her breath sharply. "How?"

"With proof of how he'd been bribing one of my employees, among other things. I strongly hinted that if I started looking, there would be other interesting aspects of Carrigan Labs' corporate operations which would come to light. He knows I don't make idle threats."

Adena let out the breath she'd been holding. She was inclined to agree with Jeff. Holt wasn't the sort of man to make idle threats. "But how did he arrange it?"

"The setup? He had his new secretary pump mine for my schedule this afternoon and then call you to arrange the 'accidental' meeting."

"Oh." Adena grimaced over her own stupidity.

"Now could we get back to my topic?" Holt inquired laconically.

"The honeymoon?" she hazarded.

"Any preferences?" he asked magnanimously.

"Well, since you ask, there's this quaint little inn up in the gold country that I've been trying to get to for the past several days..."

"Whatever you say," he murmured contentedly and reached lazily around her for the glass he'd left on the coffee table. "What the hell...?"

"What's wrong?" Adena glanced around curiously.

"Your lush of a dog just drank the rest of my sherry!"

A few days later on the night of her wedding, Adena crawled very carefully into the bed which swung from the ceiling on four long chains. It moved gently, rather like a hammock. Or a ship on a calm sea, she thought interestedly, sliding down under the covers.

A fire burned in the darkened room, a warm blaze in front of which she and Holt had just finished toasting their wedding. Max, sitting in front of the glowing coals, was unobtrusively investigating the empty champagne glasses with an inquisitive nose. He had obviously decided to branch out. He was so preoccupied with his task he didn't even glance toward the bathroom door as Holt emerged.

But Adena was fully aware of the approach of her new husband. Her eyes glowed with her love as he walked toward her, a towel wrapped around his lean waist. His sable hair was a little damp from the shower, and his tanned skin was warmed to copper in the firelight.

He came to a halt beside her, examining the picture she made ensconced in the center of the swinging bed. Adena felt herself shiver with anticipation under the impact of his deeply intent love and desire. She had never felt so wanted and so needed in her life. It left her a little breathless, feeling at once tender and passionate. She loved this man so much... Wordlessly she put out a hand to take his, and he sank down beside her, sending the bed into a small, rhythmic motion.

"Adena," he whispered huskily, holding her offered hand tightly in his own. "I love you so much that you've got me terrified."

"Terrified!" she echoed, taken aback by the unexpected remark. "Holt, what in the world do you mean? Why should you be terrified of me? You must know that I love you..."

"I know but I still worry about making the mistakes I made in the beginning," he explained heavily. "So here I sit on my wedding night, terrified of giving my wife her wedding present!"

"Wedding present? What wedding present?" she frowned at him uncomprehendingly.

He gave her a wary glance and then reached down into the bag on the floor beside the bed. Silently he handed her a small white box.

Adena accepted it, her eyes meshed with his. She saw the caution and the hope in him and smiled with inviting tenderness. Without a word she lifted off the top of the box to reveal the delicate filigree of gold inside.

"You do seem to like me in gold necklaces," she murmured softly as she lifted out the exquisite chain and fastened it around her throat.

"There's something about you in a gold necklace," he said with a laconic humor that didn't fool her for a moment. She could feel the waiting in him.

"It's beautiful, Holt," she said honestly, simply. "Thank you."

He closed his eyes briefly in relief. "Thank you, Adena." He gathered her close, his strong hands warm and captivating through the satin and lace of her dainty, low-necked nightgown.

She knew he was thanking her for accepting the gift. In a way, it was an acceptance of an aspect of him that she hadn't fully understood at first. Holt was, indeed, willing to pay for what he took in life but he was something more. He was a generous man who would want to give beautiful things to the woman he loved.

For a long moment he held her close against his heart, savoring the feel of her and the warmth of her love. They lay in silent communication and let the passion grow between them.

"It's been so long since you've shared my bed," Holt groaned roughly, one hand stroking down the length of her body to rest possessively on her thigh. The gold watch gleamed on his wrist.

"That's not exactly my fault," Adena pointed out as she arched luxuriously beneath the caress.

"I'm well aware of that. You've been quite shamelessly tempting me for days!"

"But you were so strong, so noble, so heroic…" she began mockingly, drawing her nails lightly down the skin of his shoulder.

"But maybe not so bright, hmmmm?" he drawled reflectively. "Perhaps I shouldn't have wasted so much time trying to give my wife-to-be the court-ship she once claimed she wanted. Perhaps I should have just taken what was mine anyway!'' He slipped the nightgown from her.

She sensed the exciting, sensuous menace in him and taunted him gently with her body. ''I wouldn't want you to think I'm not grateful...''

''Show me,'' he invited in soft command.

Adena did, her love pouring out of her to envelop them both as she responded to his every touch, his every kiss. But whatever she gave she received back in full measure. Holt's love was a perfect counterpart to her own.

His hands moved on her with increasing urgency, tantalizing the peaks and valleys of her body with caresses that were now excitingly arousing, now softly tempting. When she sought to return the erotic fire, he took her fingers and guided them down his flat stomach to the surging hardness of him, letting her know the effect she was already having on his body.

Trembling, she hovered over his chest, stringing quick, heated little kisses down to his waist and across his strongly muscled thigh. Her hair floated over him, drawing forth a deep, guttural groan which told her of his rising need.

He submitted to her touch, letting her explore the hardness and strength in him until she crossed some invisible barrier. Then, with a swift power that made her senses swim, Holt crushed her backward into the tangled sheets.

"I love you," he rasped, his mouth warm and damp on her skin. "I love you in all the ways it's possible for a man to love a woman. Let me give you all of me, sweetheart."

He kissed the pulse of her throat where the golden chain lay and she shivered, clutching him to her and calling out his name in soft, whispered cries of love.

He drew her hips upward, fitting her body to his with a gentleness that exploded almost at once into rippling excitement. The swinging bed moved beneath the impact of the primitive rhythm Holt set in motion.

As she lost herself in the depths of his embrace, Adena only had time for a last, fleeting thought. She revised her earlier opinion on the bed. If didn't feel so much like a boat at sea as an extension of the fantasy she always seemed to experience when Holt held her like this. She was floating in the sea itself.

Together they let the deep tides take them, and when the waves had abandoned them on a foreign shore in a delicious culmination of love, Adena and Holt continued to cling to each other, holding tight until the last of their passion had drained away.

A long time later Adena became drowsily aware of Holt's fingers on the gold at her throat. She lifted sleepy, satiated eyes to find him smiling whimsically down at her.

"Like I said," he murmured in satisfaction, "there's something about you in gold…"

"I think it's the pirate in you," she remarked, wriggling a little as she snuggled against him. "I have this depressing feeling that somewhere in an earlier lifetime you amused yourself buying slave girls."

"There would have been only one I would have given anything to own," he informed her with great certainty. "And now that I've got her I'm quite content."

"This particular slave girl is going to prove very expensive to keep happy," she warned him softly.

"What's the price of making you happy, Adena?"

"All of your love, all of your passion, all of *you!*" she told him with sudden tightness in her throat.

A slow, wicked, loving grin slashed across his face. In the firelight his gray eyes glittered with promise and love. "You have married," he pointed out as he leaned down to capture her mouth, "a very generous man."

And as Adena encircled his neck with her arms, she knew she would never lack for the only gift that really mattered to her now: Holt's love.

* * * * *

Silhouette
SPECIAL EDITION
™

SPECIAL EDITION

Stories of love and life, these powerful
novels are tales that you can identify with—
romances with "something special" added
in!

Fall in love with the stories of authors such
as **Nora Roberts, Diana Palmer, Ginna Gray**
and many more of your special favorites—as
well as wonderful new voices!

Special Edition brings you
entertainment for the heart!

SSE-GEN

SILHOUETTE® *Desire*®

Do you want...

Dangerously handsome heroes

Evocative, everlasting love stories

Sizzling and tantalizing sensuality

Incredibly sexy miniseries like **MAN OF THE MONTH**

Red-hot romance

Enticing entertainment that can't be beat!

You'll find all of this, and much *more* each and
every month in **SILHOUETTE DESIRE**. Don't miss these
unforgettable love stories by some of romance's hottest
authors. Silhouette Desire—where your fantasies will
always come true....

DES-GEN

If you've got the time...
We've got the
INTIMATE MOMENTS

Passion. Suspense. Desire. Drama. Enter a world that's larger than life, where men and women overcome life's greatest odds for the ultimate prize: love. Nonstop excitement is closer than you think...in Silhouette Intimate Moments!

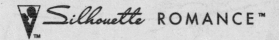

Silhouette ROMANCE™

What's a single dad to do when he needs a wife by next Thursday?

Who's a confirmed bachelor to call when he finds a baby on his doorstep?

How does a plain Jane in love with her gorgeous boss get him to notice her?

From classic love stories to romantic comedies to emotional heart tuggers, **Silhouette Romance** offers six irresistible novels every month by some of your favorite authors!
Such as…beloved bestsellers **Diana Palmer, Annette Broadrick, Suzanne Carey, Elizabeth August** and **Marie Ferrarella,** to name just a few—and some sure to become favorites!

Fabulous Fathers…Bundles of Joy…Miniseries… Months of blushing brides and convenient weddings… Holiday celebrations… You'll find all this and much more in **Silhouette Romance**—always emotional, always enjoyable, always about love!

WAYS TO *UNEXPECTEDLY* MEET MR. RIGHT:

♡ Go out with the sexy-sounding stranger your daughter secretly set you up with through a personal ad.

♡ RSVP yes to a wedding invitation—soon it might be your turn to say "I do!"

♡ Receive a marriage proposal by mail— from a man you've never met....

These are just a few of the unexpected ways that written communication leads to love in Silhouette Yours Truly.

Each month, look for two fast-paced, fun and flirtatious Yours Truly novels (with entertaining treats and sneak previews in the back pages) by some of your favorite authors—and some who are sure to become favorites.

YOURS TRULY™:
Love—when you least expect it!

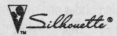

YT-GEN